PANAMA

PANAMA

AN HISTORICAL NOVEL

bill boyd

CAPITAL
BOOKS, INC.
Sterling, Virginia

Photo, p. ii: The inauguration of the Panama Canal, August 15, 1914, with the first transit of the steamship *Ancon*. *(Panama Canal Commission, Balboa, Ancon, Republic of Panama)*

Library of Congress Cataloging-in-Publication Data

  Boyd, Bill (William Young)
    Panama : an historical novel / by Bill Boyd.
    ISBN 1-892123-15-0
    1. Panama Canal (Panama) -- History Fiction. I. Title
PS3552.0884P36   1999
813'.54--dc21   99-39375
                                                        CIP
ISBN 1-892123-15-0

Printed in Canada on acid-free paper that meets the American National Standards Institute Z39-48 Standard.

Capital Books, Inc.
22883 Quicksilver Drive
Sterling, Virginia 20166

10   9   8   7   6   5   4   3   2   1

CENTRAL CHARACTERS

Manuel Amador: First leader of the Republic of Panama

Arnulfo Arias: President of the Republic of Panama (1949–1951)

Philippe Bunau-Varilla: A Frenchman, who, as representative of Panama, negotiated the first Panama Canal Treaty

Manuel Chomorro: Maria Lacayo's suitor, well-known for having a violent temper

Fred: Labor boss and friend of George Phillips

George Washington Goethals: Second Chief Engineer of the Panama Canal project

William Crawford Gorgas: Physician responsible for eradicating yellow fever, malaria, and other diseases from Panama

Juan de la Guardia: Panamanian businessman and friend of George Phillips

John Hay: U.S. Secretary of State (1901–1905) who, as representative of the United States, negotiated the first Panama Canal Treaty

Julie Kingman: Wife of Larry Kingman

Larry Kingman: Member of the Rough Riders

José Lacayo: Nicaraguan cabinet minister

Maria Lacayo: Daughter of José Lacayo

Francisco Machado: Resident of Havana

Francisco Menocal: Manager of the Inglaterra Hotel in Havana

Pepe Mora: Nicaraguan guide

John Tyler Morgan: U.S. senator from Alabama and chairman of the Senate Committee on Interoceanic Canals

George Roosevelt Phillips: Nephew of Theodore Roosevelt and member of the Rough Riders

George Roosevelt Phillips II: Son of Billy and Victoria Phillips

Sophie Wentworth Phillips: Wife of George Phillips and sister of Larry Kingman

Victoria Holmes Phillips: Wife of Billy Phillips

William "Billy" Kingman Phillips: Son of George and Sophie Phillips

Theodore Roosevelt: Commander of the Rough Riders and future president of the United States

Dean Rusk: U.S. Secretary of State (1963–1969)

John Smith: Harvard classmate of Billy Phillips

John Stevens: First Chief Engineer of the Panama Canal project

Omar Torrijos: Leader of Panama between 1968 and 1981

Admiral John Walker: Head of the Isthmian Canal Commission

Marion Wendell: George Phillips' fianceé

One summer morning in 1978, nineteen-year-old George Roosevelt Phillips II sat at his family's breakfast table studying a map of Central America, a half-eaten bowl of cereal pushed to the side. When his father appeared at the doorway, smartly dressed for his role as an officer of the State Department, George looked up and asked, "Dad, why are we giving away the Panama Canal?"

The Honorable William Phillips, who was never called anything but "Billy," smiled as he tightened his necktie in the reflection of the kitchen mirror. "America isn't *giving* the canal away, George. We never really owned it. We leased it from Panama, and now they're canceling the lease."

George looked confused. "But America built it, right?" he ventured.

"That's right, son. We did. We poured a lot of blood, sweat, and concrete into it, too."

"So why are we giving it back to Panama?"

Billy Phillips thought carefully before answering. "The Panamanians thought our original treaty wasn't satisfactory—for a lot of reasons. In fact, they were able to convince President Carter to negotiate a new treaty to eventually turn the canal and all the territory we occupied under the old agreement back to Panama. On December 31, 1999, at noon, as a matter of fact."

"The original treaty was the Bunu-Villa something, right?" said George.

"Bunau-Varilla. I'm impressed, son. I thought all those stories about your grandfather bored you to death."

"Well, a little. But I saw a show on TV about the canal and it was pretty neat. Even though I'm not directly descended from Teddy Roosevelt, it still feels good to be a distant relative of his."

Billy patted George on his shoulder. "Well, he was a great president and you should be proud of him. He really wanted that canal. He supported the Panamanian secession from Colombia. He expected to make the same treaty with Panama that Colombia rejected."

George furrowed his eyebrows in concentration.

"So," his father continued, "when this Frenchman who represented Panama offered to sign a treaty giving us everything we wanted *plus* much more than we ever expected in our wildest dreams, we took it.

"And that's the root of the problem," he continued. "We never should have fallen for the Frenchman's deal. We acted like a bunch of greedy little pigs. As Secretary Hay told your grandfather George when he signed the treaty, the deal was so good, he couldn't refuse it."

George looked up. "But don't you always say that when a deal looks too good to be true, it usually is?"

"Exactly, son. If you take advantage of somebody, it always comes back to haunt you."

The young man stood up, his breakfast finished. "Oh, well. Fair is fair, I guess. So the Panama Canal is gone. It's not the end of the world."

"Son, the canal's not gone. It's more like a kidnapped child is being returned to its rightful parents."

PART ONE

George Roosevelt Phillips was wetter and more miserable than he had ever been in his life. The downpour that had started the previous afternoon pounded on the tent's roof, threatening to make him wetter still as it crept in under the canvas like the tentacles of a giant insect. Above his head a monstrous mosquito buzzed voraciously. The damn creatures were everywhere in Cuba at the end of June 1898.

Cramped and uncomfortable, George stretched his long, lean frame as much as he could without disturbing his tentmate. Under his ratty, wool blanket Larry Kingman slept peacefully atop the log platform he had hastily constructed in a futile attempt to stay dry that long, wet night. A disheveled mass of bushy, blond hair peeked out from under the blanket. He was nearly as tall as George was with a few extra pounds around the waist he attributed to "good women, good food, and good whiskey." Larry had been a Texas cowboy before he joined Roosevelt's Rough Riders. Like thousands of other bold young Americans, Larry had eagerly joined up for the fighting in Cuba. He freely admitted he was out for the adventure—a chance to test his worth and see some of the world. Of course, he never told anyone his father owned one of the largest ranches in Texas. He liked people to think he was a "gunslinger and an outlaw," a real cowboy.

The Cuban experience was not a hardship for rough, tough Larry Kingman. He had confessed early to George in his rambling voice, "I was tired of sitting pretty, just punching cows on my daddy's spread. The West's too damned civilized these days. You shoot somebody, and damned if they don't hang you."

George smiled. For two young men from such different backgrounds, he and Larry were getting along pretty well. And Larry's friends from Arizona, New Mexico, and other parts of the "Wild West" seemed to like him too. "For a Harvard brat, you're okay," they'd told him.

George sighed. What he hadn't told them and what they hadn't guessed was that he was the nephew of their commander, Colonel Theodore Roosevelt. Nor had George told them the real reason he had volunteered for this expedition. When he thought back on those days before Cuba, he was filled with the same sorrow and confusion he'd felt before he left Boston. He still couldn't understand why his dear Marion had rejected him.

≈

He and Marion Wendell had grown up together as neighbors in Boston. Once childhood friends, they had become pen pals when George went to Andover, then dinner party and dance companions when he started at Harvard. She had a warmth and sweetness about her that would have enchanted any man. Their fondness for each other deepened as they matured into young adults, stealing kisses whenever they were left alone for a moment on a picnic or a walk in the woods. George assumed Marion was "his girl," that they would become engaged and eventually marry. Such was the way of the world at the turn of the century. His love for her grew stronger and stronger, and he was confident that their lives were already bound together, just waiting for the official union when he finished his senior year in college.

Deciding to act one evening in early spring, he invited Marion for dinner at the handsome Beacon Hill house he had inherited from his parents and now shared with his spinster aunt, Caroline, only a few streets from Marion's own prestigious address on Commonwealth Avenue. What he didn't tell her was that Aunt Caroline was away in Maine. The cook and housekeeper were out too. They were alone for the very first time in their lives.

At first, Marion seemed to enjoy being alone with him. After some cold chicken, a bottle of white burgundy, and some fresh strawberries, George sat happily on the sofa next to Marion and put his arm around her. She didn't protest. She even smiled and looked up at him. But George was sensitive enough to see the troubled look in her eyes.

He turned to face her, lifted her chin in his hand, and kissed her softly. Marion still seemed uncomfortable, but she didn't say anything. So he kissed her again. Then she was kissing him back. He kissed her neck lightly and gently began to loosen the pins from her lovely chestnut hair. But suddenly she pulled away.

Flushed and short of breath, she cried, "Stop, George! We can't let this happen! Never. You hear? It must *never* happen again."

George was shocked. Marion had never lashed out like this. She was always soft-spoken and gentle. Now she seemed tense and angry. What was wrong?

"Marion, darling, don't be so upset. You know we love each other and I'm going to ask your father for your hand the first chance I get."

Now Marion was silent. George thought she was just letting his words sink in, that she was as happy as he was. But suddenly she looked at him with a strange determination. "We had a family discussion about you last night, George. You and I have seen a lot of each other for most of our lives, and people assume we'll marry." She caught her breath. "But Mother and Dad think otherwise. They want me to see other men." She stopped, waiting for his response. He could only gape at her, too stunned to respond. "You see, George, you just aren't rich enough."

George Phillips couldn't trust himself to speak for a moment. He was flabbergasted. This couldn't be happening. Didn't she love him? Hadn't they always planned to be together?

"I–I have a small income," he stammered, more in self-defense than actual conviction. "It's not a huge fortune, but we'd be able to live comfortably for the rest of our lives on it," he repeated. "I can take up law or banking or public service or—" he mumbled, avoiding that lovely face he'd thought he knew so well. When he glanced up, he saw a new Marion before him. Cold. Resigned.

"I'm sorry, George. I have to marry a millionaire. Somebody who can give me everything I want—big houses, yachts, jewels, horses."

In confusion and despair, George gazed blankly at the spiraled, wooden trim of the red velvet sofa. This was not Marion. She had never cared for such things, anymore than he had. He knew she was forcing herself to be callous and hard-hearted. But why? He loved her, and he was sure she loved him. What had changed this sweet, gentle girl into a greedy, heartless human being?

"Marion, what is this really about?" he demanded. "You know we can be rich if we want to be. I'll just have to work harder." He was suddenly confident again. "We can make our own future! Don't you know that?" He started to reach for her again, but she pulled away defiantly.

She is plainly uncomfortable and unhappy, thought George. Then it hit him. Her father! Old Mr. Wendell wanted to use her like a medieval king used his daughters—to make a strategic alliance for his own advantage. Yes, a family alliance. He'd heard rumors about Wendell being in financial difficulties, but it must be worse than he'd thought. But what the hell? George's family was as well-connected as any. No, Marion's father must have another suitor in mind, and Marion must go along with his choice. It was the only explanation. What could he do? How could he convince her? He looked into her eyes and saw only deep sorrow and determination.

George realized her father had pulled up the drawbridge and locked the gates against him. "All right," he said, suddenly resigned, "I won't prolong your anguish. You must feel some sort of duty to your family, and I can't force you to marry me. It breaks my heart, but I'll let you go." He extended his hand and grasped hers, knowing it would be the last time they touched as lovers. Now they must be just family friends.

Her voice trembled as she said, "Tonight never happened. We never kissed like that."

"No. Nothing happened."

Without warning, Marion put her arms around George and hugged him hard. She looked up and said, "No matter what happens, George, remember that I loved you very much. I have no control over my life anymore."

That was all she said, and he couldn't think of anything else to say. He walked her home along the deserted street in silence. The gaslight lamp over her chiseled oak door made Marion's face ghostlike as she looked sadly into his face, said goodbye, and turned into her house.

George returned home, gazing up at the crescent moon partially obscured by clouds. Damn! he thought. Why won't Marion stand up to her father? She loves *me*! He pictured Marion's father in his mind— pompous and bald, a typical Boston banker, bright but not always astute as far as business was concerned. But Mrs. Wendell was usually able to handle him. She was a serene, pleasant lady, still beautiful and very kind. How could *she* let this happen? How could all of them destroy a love that was so good, so right?

George took the next train out of Boston, leaving behind everything he had known: family, friends, Harvard, and especially Marion. He carried a small valise along with a copy of the latest Hearst dispatch. The newspaper featured a bold headline urging America's patriotic youth to answer the call of their country and defeat the Spanish and free neighboring Cuba. Like the hand of fate, the newspaper had beckoned him when he returned forlorn and dejected from Marion's that night. He knew in his heart he was running away from a situation he could not endure—living in the same city with Marion and her future husband, whoever he might be. Perhaps he was simply running away. It didn't seem to matter. With newfound resolution, he decided to strive with every fiber of his being to show them all, to seek a new future without Marion.

Two weeks later, he found himself a private soldier in the First U.S. Volunteer Cavalry. During those first weeks of hard training, he reflected on the progress of his life so far. He came to the self-pitying conclusion that fate had led him inexorably to his present unenviable position. Jonathan Phillips, George's father, had never succeeded in anything he attempted. Most of the money he inherited he squandered in failed ventures. He began to drink heavily and one night did not come home. Two days later, a couple of hikers found his body in the woods with a pistol in his hand and a bullet in his head.

George's mother was a sweet, devout, "God Help Us" type of woman. She died shortly after they found her husband's body. George was devastated, and only fifteen. Luckily his mother had provided him with an inheritance. He spent holidays from Andover alternating between the Beacon Hill home with Aunt Caroline and the home of another aunt and uncle who always treated him sympathetically. *Too* sympathetically, as if he were an orphan, which he was but didn't want to be reminded of every minute of the day. So, he ran away. Got as far as Hartford, when he ran out of money and had to cable his uncle, who came to get him. He felt ashamed, degraded. He turned inward and tried to analyze his feelings toward his late parents. Was he really forlorn? Was he sad and grieving? No. He felt neutral toward his father, he decided. Neither loved nor hated him. Father had just *been there*—once in awhile. And his mother? She was wrapped up in herself and her misfortune in marrying the likes of Jonathan Phillips. All of her sympathy was really for herself, not for him. George decided he hadn't really liked her either. She hadn't given him the love he needed. These thoughts made him feel guilty. They were unworthy. A person is supposed to love his parents. He was the one who must have failed in some way. Marion was the last straw. Yes, he was right to have left Boston.

Now in Cuba, on the eve of battle, he had even bleaker thoughts. He had already fought in a few skirmishes against the Spanish, including the ambush at Las Guásimas, but had not been where the fighting was heavy. He had heard gunfire, seen a few Spaniards, shot at them, probably missed, and that was that, although men were killed at Las Guásimas. His friend, Hamilton Fish, was one of the first. Hamilton was five years older than George, but they were chums. Hamilton's grandfather had been in Lincoln's cabinet, but now Ham was dead and tomorrow there was going to be a big battle.

Nobody had to tell him. The preparations told the story without words. What if he lost his nerve? What if he ran? Unthinkable. Was he prepared to die, as Fish had, in battle? In his sick mental condition he relished the idea of Marion's suffering and regret when she received the news that he had been killed. She would probably swoon, he gloated, and need years to recuperate. Great. Except the part about his getting killed. Not so great. Maybe he'd survive. Maybe he'd be wounded. His mind raced.

Larry and his other cowboy friends had taught him to keep his head down, aim and squeeze the trigger of his Krag or his revolver. He was in excellent physical shape. Yes. He had to think more positively. He might just make it through the battle. I can do this, he resolved. But despite his best efforts, he couldn't keep his hands from shaking or his stomach from knotting up. The monotony of the rainy night was broken with urgent, half-hour ventures out into the rain to relieve himself.

Despite his newfound comrades, George hated the life of a soldier. The ground was muddy, insects swarmed at night, and there was always the danger of getting fatally ill. Added to that, he was in a cavalry regiment that had no horses. They'd had to leave them behind in Tampa before boarding the ships to Cuba. The only good part of being in the army was that, although he still didn't realize it, he'd picked up the "common touch." His best friends in the outfit were not the high-born aristocrats of Boston, but rough and ready "cowboys" from the Wild West. He would have liked to have been an officer, but not many of his friends were, and he knew his uncle would never give him a commission. Such nepotism was unthinkable.

What still bothered him the most, even as he tried to compose himself for a battle that might be his last, was Marion's rejection. He just knew there had to be something dreadfully wrong. She just wouldn't have done this on her own. He was still hurt and puzzled. "Not rich enough?" He just couldn't understand it. If she loved him—and she said she did—why wouldn't she marry him?

"You're thinking about Marion again," Larry whispered. "Go to sleep, George."

The next day, not rested but determined to be brave, twenty-year-old George Roosevelt Phillips stood tall in his new uniform. Lean, without an ounce of fat, he looked even taller than his already sizeable six-foot-two-inch frame. His hair was blond but receding and rather thin on top, which made him seem older than his years, a source of great embarrassment to him. He didn't realize that most people didn't care. His nose was sharp and well-formed, his lips well-shaped, and his violet-blue eyes twinkled with intelligence, characteristics that had drawn Marion to him since their childhood. The truth was that Marion Wendell should never have listened to her father. She plainly loved George, but he didn't know this.

"Patrician" aptly described George though he had been accepted as one of the "boys" in his few months with the Rough Riders. And he was learning to be a diplomat. He had a chameleon-like flair for language. Like the worldly Europeans, he could shift from one language to another, switching effortlessly from one U.S. geographic accent to another. When he was bantering with the other men, he could speak effortlessly in their Western drawl, telling tall tales with the best of them. In the next moment, he could shift back into the cultured, subdued accent of an Eastern university graduate.

Suddenly he was in the midst of what later came to be known as the Battles of Kettle Hill and San Juan Hill. George had no idea where he was or what he was doing. He followed orders. He saw his friends fall, but he didn't stop to help them. That was against orders. He kept moving ahead into the hail of bullets whizzing over him, beside him, kicking mud on him as they hit the ground at his feet. The shrapnel from exploding artillery shells narrowly missed him, and he paused only to fire at the unseen enemy. He moved forward until he met the Spaniards close-in. Now he was into their lines. Enemy soldiers were shooting at him at point-blank range, swinging their knives and lunging with their bayonets. Some of the Rough Riders seemed to love using bayonets and knives, but George used his rifle as a club, swinging it this way and that until he broke the stock. Bending to pick up the broken rifle, he saw a Spanish soldier standing over him, his long cane knife raised to hack George to death. Luckily, he was able to clear his revolver from its holster in a flash and shoot the man dead. Afterward, he continued to use the pistol as his weapon of choice during the close-in fighting, even though he was able to salvage an intact Krag-Jorgenson rifle from a fallen trooper.

Uncle Ted seemed to be all over the battlefield, astride his horse, Little Texas. How can they miss hitting him? thought George. Roosevelt now commanded the Rough Riders. When he had formed the First Volunteer Cavalry, he'd given the command to his old friend, Colonel Leonard Wood, since Wood was an experienced combat soldier who had fought the Apaches and earned a Medal of Honor. Now Wood had taken command of a brigade and appointed Roosevelt leader of the Rough Riders.

Again the command rang out—"CHARGE!"—and again George found himself running toward the oncoming enemy bullets. He'd run forward, then fall to the ground and roll over. It made him a more difficult target. The Spanish had Mauser rifles, which were far superior to the Krags. And the smokeless powder they used disguised their positions. George knew he had to outsmart them, since he couldn't outshoot them. Larry Kingman flopped onto the ground beside him. "A lot of the boys are down," he panted.

"Don't tell me who," said George. "We've still got to get to the top of that damned hill. Tell me later."

They lay there catching their breath for a minute. "I think the closer we get, the higher we'll be on the hill, and the harder we'll be to hit because the enemy can't depress their machine guns and artillery pieces that sharply," said George. "Understand what I mean?"

"Let's get going," said Larry.

A drenaline flowing, the two troopers ran as if they were in a foot race. Straight up the hill, they passed other soldiers, never pausing to dive for cover. They ran, up and up Kettle Hill. George knew he was sprinting forward so fast because he was scared to death, and sprinting somehow kept his mind off of the reality he faced. At least he was running toward the enemy, not running away. Now, they were almost on top of a German-type machine gun. It was aimed at their left. George rose and fired an entire cylinder from his pistol into the machine gun crew, toward their blind side. Larry, in turn, did the same. They both jumped into the machine gun pit at the same time. The gunners were all dead. George and Larry commandeered the equipment, turning the machine gun toward the Spanish positions. "Do you know how to work this thing?" shouted George. It was quite different from the old Gatling guns they knew.

"Never even saw one before."

George crouched behind the gun. Bullets were singing all around him. He analyzed the machine. There was a belt, half used, in the breech. If it was firing when they killed the gunners, it was in position to fire now. He aimed at the large house in front of them and squeezed the trigger. Both he and Larry jumped as the gun began to chatter loudly. Then, George realized they were drawing enemy fire. It was all concentrated on *them* now. But this was giving the rest of the Rough Riders a chance to move forward faster, which they wasted no time in doing.

A few seconds later, both George and Larry were hit several times by enemy small-arms fire. As the other surviving Rough Riders swept past them, George took bodily stock. His right leg hurt and blood was seeping through his trousers. His neck was bleeding but only grazed. His vision was completely blurred from a pool of blood flooding his eyes. He wiped his forehead with the back of his hand. It stung. "I'm a goner, Larry," he managed to gasp. "They shot my head off."

No answer.

"Larry? Larry? You there?"

Still no answer.

George felt the ground grow wetter beneath his head. This was it. He was going to die. Larry was probably already dead. The curious thing was, thought George, that he hadn't even felt the Spanish bullets hit him. But they'd hit him all right, knocked him off balance, taken off his head or most of it. And now he was practically a dead man. Funny. Just when he'd changed his mind about dying, too.

George groped in his trouser pocket and drew out a damp handkerchief, which he used to wipe his forehead and eyes in an unsuccessful attempt to clear his vision. Damn! he thought. He couldn't catch his breath, not perhaps from his own wounds but from the penetrating fear over Larry's fate. He reached out. No Larry. The pandemonium of battle raged on. Yells and shouting swelled the air. Explosions and rifle fire everywhere.

"Here he is!" George heard Larry's familiar drawl and felt the hand of the medical corpsman trying to wipe away the gobs of blood on his forehead.

"Can you open your eyes?" asked the medic.

"I'll try," croaked George. He forced them halfway open and discovered he could actually see. "Is there anything left of my head?" he asked tentatively.

"You'll be all right. Head wounds bleed to beat all hell."

"How about the rest of me?" George could feel strange hands on his leg and a bandage wiping his neck.

"Leg's all you have to worry about. Doctor'll have to see it."

George didn't feel like answering. Instead, he said, "Larry, I saw you get hit, too. I thought you were dead. How are you doing? And thanks for getting help for me."

"Those Mauser bullets went right through me. Didn't hit anything but my canteen and my ass."

"My leg, Larry. How bad is it? Don't let them cut off my leg."

Larry reached down and gripped George's hand. He hesitated, "I won't let them unless it's absolutely necessary to save your life."

Another man had joined them. "How is he?" he asked. "My nephew. How is he? He looks bad." The other men had snapped to attention the minute Colonel Roosevelt arrived.

"I think he'll be all right, sir," said the medic. "But we won't know until the doctors see him."

George's eyes were fully open now. He smiled. "Hi, Uncle Ted," he said huskily.

Roosevelt flashed the famous tooth-baring smile. "I saw what you and Larry did today! I'll never forget it, George, Larry. Never! You were both magnificent, a credit to the regiment, a credit to your country. I'm putting you and every other man in the outfit in for medals. I'm also promoting you two to lieutenants, effective immediately."

"Thank you, sir," said the two in unison.

"Just think," said Roosevelt, "you'll be able to tell your children and grandchildren you were commissioned on the battlefield for displaying exemplary courage under enemy fire!"

"*If* we make it," said George, his gloom returning like the twilight after a sunny day.

"If you make it? George, I'm tempted to kick your ass from here to Santiago! Of course you'll make it, you damned fool." Then the colonel's voice softened. "You could have gotten killed so easily today. So easily. No more heroics, Nephew. Next adventure, you stay home." He patted George on the shoulder and continued on.

≈

Lieutenants Phillips and Kingman received their medals at Camp Wikoff on Long Island, New York, where the Rough Riders, one of the most famous units in U.S. military history, mustered out of the service. George Phillips was left with a slight but permanent limp from the bullet wound in his leg. The only other visible reminders of the battle were hairline scars across his forehead and along his neck.

Before they parted, George made a request of Larry: "Look, nobody knows where the Wendells went. 'West' to them could mean Texas. So if you hear anything, please drop me a note. I *have* to know where they are."

"You have my word," said Larry.

After his experiences in the Spanish-American War, a new, more mature George Phillips returned to Harvard and graduated with honors. It was now 1900. A few weeks after graduation ceremonies he caught an overnight train to Washington to visit his uncle, Teddy Roosevelt, who welcomed him warmly. "George!" he greeted his nephew. "I couldn't be more delighted you've come to visit your old uncle."

"My young uncle, you mean." George smiled. "What are you now, forty-one? forty-two?"

Roosevelt returned the grin without responding directly. "Well, I feel like an old uncle. As vice president, I don't have a lot of responsibility in the running of the government. President McKinley decides everything important. I just cut the ribbons on new bridges, dedicate buildings—that kind of thing."

"Well, that sounds like fun," said George. "Let me know if you need an assistant. I'm trying to decide what I'm going to do, and I've come to ask your advice."

The vice president sat down behind his desk and offered George a chair. "One of the projects I am interested in is the canal between the Atlantic and Pacific Oceans," said Roosevelt. "Everybody's talking about it."

George nodded. "I understand Great Britain has signed a treaty with us giving the United States exclusive rights to build a canal across Central America."

"It will be built in Nicaragua, of course," said Roosevelt. "That's been decided already. But a lot of other details haven't. Ever been to Nicaragua, George?"

"No, sir." Phillips shook his head.

"How would you like to go?"

George didn't hesitate. "Very much, sir."

Roosevelt strode over to a table and pulled out a map of Central America. As he and George stood over it, the vice president went over the plan for the Nicaraguan canal. "Look," he pointed. "Here's the San Juan River. It'll need dredging. But then we have Lake Nicaragua and Lake Managua, both usable. Then we dredge out this little piece of land on the Atlantic, and, by damn, we have our canal!"

"It looks almost too easy," said George.

"Looks are deceiving, George. I'll arrange for you to meet first with Admiral John Walker, the head of the nine-man Isthmian Canal Commission. He's very influential and can fill you in."

George found Admiral Walker to be a most imposing figure. He knew that Walker was known around Washington as "The Old Man of the Sea." Dressed in civilian clothes, he was a large, handsome man who carried himself with military style. His gray hair was parted right down the middle and his cheeks were adorned with thick, mutton chop whiskers. Self-important yet direct and unaffected, Admiral Walker had a reputation for integrity.

"As you know, young man, I'm not an engineer," said Walker.

"Yes, sir."

"Therefore, I never attempt a technical role. I rely on others to do that part, and I weigh the evidence and decide the best course to take."

"Yes, sir," said George again. "I think that's a wise policy, sir."

"I like your attitude, young fellow. You'll do." After a short discussion with the admiral, George was instructed to go over the Nicaraguan area, evaluate it, look for problems and ways to solve them. Cornelius Vanderbilt had built a working railroad there and his vessels navigated Lake Nicaragua regularly. George was given government credentials and told to report to the U.S. Minister to Nicaragua.

≈

In Managua, Nicaragua, the U.S. Minister to Nicaragua held an elaborate dinner for his distinguished guest, George Phillips. Dinner guests included a Nicaraguan cabinet minister, José Lacayo, and his lovely daughter, Maria. George found Maria graceful and charming. Her English was good, since her father had been an ambassador to the United States and she had lived in Washington for a few years. They discovered there were a lot of people they both knew, and they spent much of the evening in conversation. George explained to Maria that he had to go into the country to look at the canal route but hoped to see her when he returned. She seemed pleased and smiled shyly.

After dinner, Maria's father took George aside. "I'm glad to see you and Maria are getting friendly. She's become involved with a most undesirable young man named Manuel Chomorro, the 'black sheep' of an otherwise fine family. He spends his time gambling and drinking and is entirely unsuitable for my daughter. I hope you'll be able to distract her. But be careful!" Señor Lacayo told George. He laughed, then added more seriously, "What I mean is, Manuel is a very dangerous man. They say he has killed several men who displeased him."

"By 'several,' you mean—?" asked George.

"Oh, twenty, or perhaps thirty," replied Lacayo.

CHAPTER

6

The next day, George hired an old renegade, Pepe Mora, as his guide and set out to inspect the probable route of the proposed canal, even though nobody was certain where it would be. In the weeks he spent examining various lakes, mountain regions, and cattle pastures, he began to love the country. It was beautiful, much like the western part of the United States. Nicaragua was mostly cattle and farm country, sparsely populated. The ranches were far from each other, and the towns were small, no more than villages in most cases. Managua, of course, was the capital and was larger. Rivas, Leon, and Masaya were provincial and delightful but very rough-and-ready Spanish in their architecture. The ranchers dressed much as they did in the American West, with revolvers at their hips. Their horses were strong but small.

George extracted as much Nicaraguan history as he could from his colorful old guide. "I fight with Walker," said Pepe casually one day.

"Who?"

"You no know about William Walker?"

George shook his head. Mora frowned.

"Walker come here from U.S. in '55 maybe. Bring a lot of gun-toters to fight in one of our revolutions. But, in truth, come to take Nicaragua.

Big battle at Rivas. You never see so much smoke and shooting. Lots of dead, I tell you. Walker win. That's when I join Walker."

George cocked his head. "Why would you do that?" he asked.

"I like to live, señor. Walker shoot a lot of what he call *bandidos*. Then Walker get himself elected El Presidente. President Walker, he is. In Rivas, anyhow."

George was silent for a few minutes. "Why did Walker try to take Nicaragua?" he asked.

The old man scratched his head. "He want bring Nicaragua into the United States." He paused to ponder. "Walker from south in United States. Want to bring Nicaragua into States as 'slave state.' Is right word, señor? You understand, señor?"

George nodded.

"Big mistake," said Pepe Mora.

"I agree, but why?"

Pepe scratched his head again. "Nicaragua no have slaves," he ventured.

George laughed out loud.

"So," continued Mora, "Walker make law: Nicaragua must have slaves."

George laughed again. If Pepe Mora hadn't been so serious, he would have thought he was pulling his leg.

"That big mistake. Everybody angry. Then Walker make second big mistake."

George shook his head. "What could that have been?"

"President Walker take away Señor Vanderbilt's license to do business in Nicaragua."

"What?" exclaimed George. "Walker must have been crazy."

Pepe nodded. "Señor Vanderbilt, he get damn mad, you bet! Walker get two *gringos* to try to take over his business but no pay him nothing for it. You know what Vanderbilt write?

"No."

"He say, 'I not sue you. Law take too long. I going ruin you.'"

George chuckled. "What happened?"

"People rise up against Walker 'cause no like slavery. Vanderbilt send in Costa Rican army to join people to fight Walker. Walker run away to U.S. gunboat and they take him home to U.S.A."

"And the two fellows who double-crossed Vanderbilt?"

"He ruin them," replied Pepe Mora casually.

Phillips was thinking. Wow! An American president of Nicaragua, even if he was a freebooter. "So what happened to Walker?"

"Like I say, he go back States. Then make other big mistake. He return to Central America with another band of adventurers. He get beat. Go back to New Orleans. Come back here. Hondurans catch him. Firing squad shoot him."

"When?"

"Catch him September 11. Firing squad shoot him September 12."

"What year?"

"1860."

"How do you know all this? How can you remember the dates and all that?"

"We make big *fiesta* when we find out. For next five years we have big *fiestas* every September 11 and 12. I know year because the big American war end in 1865. So! Walker die in 1860."

George didn't question his guide's logic. What the heck? He made a mental note to learn more about William Walker for himself.

Besides chatting with Pepe, George was taking notes on everything. He found the country lovely, the deep volcanic lakes turquoise and pure. It was said there were freshwater sharks in Lake Managua! The lakes in the possible canal area would save a lot of digging time and could be used as Commodore Vanderbilt had used them in his Trans-Nicaraguan Transport Company. In fact, using the San Juan River and the two lakes, there would be a minimum amount of excavation required. If it hadn't been for William Walker, Vanderbilt would probably have dug out the remaining sections and built his own canal. Still, something in the beautiful landscape bothered George, but he couldn't put his finger on exactly what it was.

≈

At an American Legation dinner several weeks later, George asked the minister, "Have you ever heard of a man named William Walker?"

The small entourage in the room fell silent, as if somebody had said something terribly out of line. Unfazed, the minister replied in his ordinary tone of voice, "Oh, yes. He was a renegade American. Came to Nicaragua during the civil wars in the '50s, picked what he thought was the winning side and fought for them. Then he took over and made himself president. Didn't last long. Ended up in front of a firing squad, which is exactly what he deserved."

The minister had said the right thing. There was an almost audible sigh of relief throughout the room. One man said, "Walker was president in *Rivas*. He was *never* president of Nicaragua."

"Shush," said his wife. "We're not going over all this again."

CHAPTER

Dressing for dinner at the Lacayo's, George read again the now dog-eared, faded letter he had received from Aunt Caroline soon after the battle of San Juan Hill. Written in his aunt's polite, proper diction, the gist was that the Wendells' bank had gone broke, and Mr. Wendell had planned, as a last resort, to save the family's fortune by marrying Marion to a very rich New Yorker.

"I was right!" thought George. The Wendells' future depended on the match. The fact that the suitor was overweight, nearly fifty, and had the manners of a pig were merely inconveniences to suffer and overcome. Still, Mrs. Wendell, "poor thing," hadn't wanted to have the wedding in Boston where the groom would have been exposed to the scrutiny of her family and friends. A quiet, immediate, family-only ceremony would take place in New York.

The night before the happy event, the big man's friends gave him a dinner party, and he got so drunk he passed out. Since he often did that, his friends, laughing and joking, left him where he was and reeled out of the restaurant. He was still there when the busboys started to clean up the place around one in the morning. Knowing who he was, they simply mopped around him until one of them took a closer look and found he had died. There was a certain amount of consternation, of course, but there it was. Dead with an empty port bottle clutched in one hand and a cigar butt in the other.

The Wendells decided to leave Boston. With the little money they had left, they boarded a train to Missouri. One of Mrs. Wendell's close friends received a letter from her written from St. Louis saying they were going still further west.

Of course! That explained Marion's bizarre behavior, George thought. She loved him and wanted him, but she had chosen family duty instead.

Closing his aunt's letter, he wondered if he'd ever see Marion again.

≈

There were many prominent Nicaraguans at the Lacayo's dinner party, and George liked them all. The group consisted chiefly of owners of large ranches and farms, a banker or two, several lawyers, and many government officials. George was in the middle of a joke with a Nicaraguan engineering authority when Maria came over with a young man and said, "Oh, *Jorge,* have you met Manuel Chomorro?"

Chomorro was dark, with coal black hair and a sharp nose like George's. He was well-built but compact, about five-feet-six-inches tall. His eyes were so black, he didn't seem to have any pupils. And they flashed, in contrast to George's which glittered. This man could kill without a moment's hesitation, thought George.

"I've heard of you," said George, without emotion.

"I've heard of you, too," Chomorro answered coolly. "I am not impressed."

Despite the obvious mutual dislike, George was surprised at Chomorro's rudeness. It was then that he noticed that the group he had been talking to before Maria and Manuel arrived had moved to the other side of the room. They either don't like Manuel or they are afraid of him, thought George.

At dinner, he sat next to Maria and flirted with her during the meal. She was, as he had noticed earlier, a most charming young lady. His attention was so focused on Maria, he failed to notice Manuel seated far down the table. Chomorro was glaring at him with an expression of sheer hatred.

≈

In answer to his discreet questions afterwards, George discovered that young Chomorro had inherited a mean streak from his mother who came from a rather nasty, upperclass family. After Manuel killed a Chomorro ranchhand over a horse dispute, his father disinherited him and threw him out of the house. Everybody was afraid Manuel would one day return to kill his father, but the senior Chomorro had died peacefully in bed. By that time, Manuel was a greatly feared killer. Most people stayed as far away from him as possible—including officers of the law. He intimidated every man with whom he came into contact, but the ladies all adored him for some reason. Perhaps his reputation as a tough character appealed to them. His choice, though, was Maria Lacayo. She was beautiful and very rich—and she gloried in being Manuel Chomorro's sweetheart, the envy of the other bored, rich, young women of her set.

CHAPTER

8

In a field near Managua, George Phillips was target practicing with the new revolver he had just purchased. Since everybody in Nicaragua had one or two pistols holstered on his cartridge belt, George decided it would be prudent for him to do the same. He was glad he'd stuck with the cowboys and gunslingers when he served in the Rough Riders. They had taught him a lot: how to stay low, how to aim and then squeeze the trigger, never to hurry. "The gunmen who drew too fast are all buried in Boot Hill now," they had told him. "Just aim straight and squeeze."

As a result, George had little difficulty hitting the bottles he was using as targets. One by one, he smashed them all. As he reloaded for the fourth time, he heard footsteps behind him. Snapping the loaded cylinder back into the revolver, he turned his head slowly. Manuel Chomorro stood behind him.

"Learning how to use a *pistola*?" he asked.

"No. I already know how to use a *pistola*, thank you."

"I don't like you," said Chomorro. "You talk to Maria again, and I blow your head off."

George knew he couldn't let Chomorro get away with threatening him or he'd bully him every time he saw him; and George would soon be a laughingstock. "I'll speak to whomever I like, whenever I like," said George, turning slowly toward Chomorro, his pistol ready.

Chomorro felt threatened. It showed for an instant on his face. Then he drew his pistol and took a fast shot at George. He had pulled the weapon so fast, the barrel went far too high, and the bullet sang harmlessly over George's head. George aimed squarely at Chomorro's chest and squeezed the trigger. Chomorro was knocked backward several feet and hit the ground, dead.

George was in a panic. He took the first ship out of Nicaragua without returning to Managua. He knew he'd shot Chomorro in self-defense, but, without witnesses, who would believe him? Especially in Nicaragua. Then, he remembered how people felt about Chomorro and figured they probably *would* believe him. But he decided not to chance it. He regretted that decision later.

The ship he took was bound for Panama for repairs. A month in Nicaragua had changed George Roosevelt Phillips from a detached, intellectual man of leisure into a killer on the run.

≈

Alone in Panama, George decided he could distract himself and impress his uncle by examining the French equipment left over from their failed attempt to build a canal there, under the famous Count Ferdinand de Lesseps, who had successfully built the Suez Canal. George discovered that de Lesseps' French Panama Canal Company had accomplished far more than was commonly known. A lot of their equipment was still usable. The railroad, built in 1849 by American entrepreneurs Henry Aspinwall, Henry Chauncey, and John Lloyd Stephens, was a solid asset.

But in Panama malaria, yellow fever, and other deadly diseases had decimated the French. John Lloyd Stephens, the famous archeologist and financier who had discovered the Mayan ruins in Honduras and become the first president of the Panama Railroad, had also died of yellow fever on the Isthmus of Panama.

George made friends with a Panamanian named Juan de la Guardia. They enjoyed chatting together. In a quiet moment one evening, George told Juan about Cuba and San Juan Hill and the reason he limped slightly. Juan told him the story of Ran Runnells, the Texas Ranger whom the Panama Overland Freight Company hired and brought to Panama in the gold-rush days—when the Panama Railroad was still being built—to stop the dreadful pillage that local bandits were wreaking on the mule trains. The awful death toll among the mule drivers from the guns of the outlaws was making such employment as fearsome as the diseases.

First Runnells set up a transportation office to solicit freight. He slowly began hiring. The men he employed were mostly foreigners—Mexicans, Cubans, a few South Americans. They were hard men, and Runnells tested them several times to make sure they were honest and to weed out the ones with any ties to the *bandidos*. Then he acted swiftly. One morning, the citizens of Panama City woke up to find twenty-eight men hanging from the lampposts in the main plaza. Then, two weeks later, another mule train was hijacked and five men killed. It was an act of desperate bravado. One week later, eighteen more outlaws were found dangling dead from the old sea wall. The banditry suddenly ceased. By the time Runnells went home to Texas, the railroad was in operation.

George remarked, "This certainly is a colorful place. It has a lot more history than Nicaragua. It's more vibrant, more Latin American. I understand Panama voluntarily joined Simón Bolívar's Gran Colombia after you achieved your own independence, so you're really a part of South America."

"That's what makes us unique," said de la Guardia. "I know you Americans have already decided to build your canal in Nicaragua. But you should know that the French want $109 million for their equipment and their concession."

"What!" exclaimed George. "I didn't know that."

"Oh, yes. That's the reason there was no contest. In Nicaragua, you do not have to buy out anybody."

George knew that three sites had been considered: Tehuantepec in Mexico, the Nicaraguan route, and Panama. The Isthmian Canal Commission already had discarded Tehuantepec. And Nicaragua seemed to be favored over Panama.

"Have they seen all that's been done here already?" asked George.

"Yes. But the equipment, the railroad, and the concessions all belong to the French, and $109 million is too much to ask for what they have here. The French ran out of money and got caught bribing French government officials and the press. Everybody thinks the *Compagnie Universelle du Canal Interocéanique* was nothing but a big fraud to rob the French people of their savings and put money in the promoters' own pockets."

"That can't be true," said George. "They spent it here. I can see what they invested." He paused, "Some of it probably got skimmed off, but it looks to me like most of it went into equipment, buildings, and the attempted construction of a real, honest-to-God canal. I think it was just a much more difficult job than they ever dreamed it would be. Because he succeeded with the Suez Canal, the great Ferdinand de Lesseps thought his fame and reputation were all that were needed to complete this one. He came here in the dry season and never expected the torrential rains or horrendous mudslides that the nine-month rainy season brings. Now the jungle is taking over. In five years, there won't be anything left."

"How about the railroad?" ventured de la Guardia.

"At $109 million, it would be the most expensive forty-five-mile railroad in the world!"

De la Guardia simply nodded his head. "The French concession in Panama runs out in a few years. Why not be patient?"

George thought for a moment, then shook his head slowly. "I'm afraid, my friend, that Americans are not a patient people."

CHAPTER

9

George tried to make a rough inventory of the French equipment. He also reviewed the terrain. There he found problems. The Chagres River in flood was awesome. There was a twenty-two-foot tide on the Pacific side of the isthmus with a one-foot tide on the Atlantic. He appreciated the fact that the continental divide ran down Panama like a spine, but there was an earthen ridge—or "saddle"—in it, and the saddle was only twelve miles from Panama City. Still, he didn't have the experience and equipment to take soundings. Underneath the jungle growth, the soil could be soft or it could be solid rock. And, unlike Nicaragua where George saw nothing but grasslands, Panama had some of the densest jungle in the world.

His assessment completed, George prepared to return to the United States. Just as he was boarding the ship to New York, a representative of the Nicaraguan government accompanied by Juan de la Guardia and several other individuals he recognized as prominent officials of Panama intercepted him on the dock. George Phillips could almost feel the noose around his neck. He sucked in his breath. "What can I do for you, gentlemen?" he asked, trying to remain calm.

The Nicaraguan bowed. "We have come to bring you news, Señor Phillips. The body of Manuel Chomorro was found near Managua. It was about the same time you departed from Nicaragua, Señor Phillips."

George nodded, his heart in his throat.

"Tell us about it, señor, and we shall tell you what has happened since your departure from Nicaragua."

Taking a deep breath, George spoke as calmly as he could, "Manuel and I had what you might call a duel. He fired first. I fired in self-defense. He missed. I did not."

The Nicaraguan nodded. "That is exactly what the court found when they tried you in absentia. You should have reported the incident to the police and not fled like a criminal. But you see, we are not a prejudiced people. We noted that Manuel's pistol had been fired. We assumed you fired back in self-defense. A farmer nearby saw the whole thing and corroborated it. You are now officially acquitted. Go with God."

The Nicaraguan nodded once again, but this time he extended his hand and shook George's. Both smiled broadly.

George offered to buy drinks for all, and his invitation was readily accepted. Leaving the dockside cantina, it was a very merry group of men who escorted George on board the New York-bound ship. Just before sailing, George told Juan, "God, what good luck! I felt like kissing that Nicaraguan."

"Of course," said Juan. "That's how they want you to feel. You don't think they'd treat you so nicely if they didn't know you were the nephew of Vice President Roosevelt, do you?"

"What's that got to do with it?"

"The United States is going to build a canal across Central America, probably in Nicaragua, but we hope Panama is still a possibility. I can assure you that convicting the nephew of the American vice president of murder and hanging him would greatly prejudice Nicaragua's chances."

De la Guardia patted his friend on the shoulder. "You know, George," he said, "just because the Nicaraguans are farmers and ranchers, people underestimate them. But, believe me, George, they are very shrewd."

"Amen," said George.

George arrived back in the United States in early 1901. He spent a few days in New York compiling his findings before taking the train to Washington to report to his uncle. Roosevelt was pleased with George's summary, even though it was somewhat unprofessional. "That's what I like!" exclaimed Roosevelt. "Plain English. Not a lot of technical hocus-pocus." He read some parts of the document to himself, while George stood before his desk. "I'm glad you took the opportunity to see Panama. You seem to favor it," he said, looking questioningly at George.

"Yes and no," said George.

"Please explain, my dear nephew."

"The Nicaraguan route is much longer, but Nicaragua is closer to the States. And we can incorporate the lakes and the rivers.

"Panama is shorter by far, and there's been a lot of work done by the French, a lot of equipment still in place. But the French want too much money for what there is. And the jungle there is impenetrable."

Roosevelt nodded vigorously. "Well summarized, George. I think Admiral Walker's commission will formally recommend a Nicaraguan canal. But I wanted your opinion. That's why I sent you down. Plans and rumors were flying around here so fast, I decided I'd get somebody I trusted to go down and get me some first-hand knowledge of the situation. You've done that, George. Good going, I say! Bully!"

"I killed a man in Nicaragua, Uncle Ted."

Roosevelt remained uncharacteristically silent.

"It was in self-defense, and I was acquitted of all responsibility." He then went on to tell Roosevelt the whole story of what happened.

At the end of George's narrative, the vice president nodded. Then he smiled broadly, "Thank God you're a sure shot, George. I think I'll make you one of my bodyguards, if I ever require any. You are a firecracker, nephew."

George felt better for having told his uncle the story. Then he frowned. The word "firecracker" had brought back his memories of Nicaragua. Suddenly, he realized what had been bothering him about the Nicaraguan terrain. "Uncle Ted, please don't discard Panama completely yet. Nicaragua has one fatal flaw."

"Oh? I thought you just told me it was the perfect route. What's the so-called fatal flaw?"

"In Nicaragua I saw an awful lot of volcanoes. They weren't erupting or anything like that, but they were there. And if they do erupt, the earthquakes they'll set off will destroy your canal. That, my dear uncle, is a fatal flaw."

The two men sat in silence. Vice President Roosevelt might have been irrepressible at times, but he was usually cautious, considering issues thoroughly. "Did you see any volcanoes in Panama?"

"None. At least none anywhere near the canal route. Somebody told me there were volcanoes far to the west, close to the Costa Rican border, but none where we intend to build. By the way, sir, you forgot to ask me if any of the Nicaraguan volcanoes were active."

"Are they?"

"Yes. There's one particularly nasty one called Momotombo right in the middle of Lake Nicaragua. That means it's right on the canal route. My friends confirm Momotombo is an active volcano."

Roosevelt was thoughtful. "Senator John Tyler Morgan is a friend of mine. He's chairing the Senate Committee on Interoceanic Canals. They call it the Morgan Committee. He and everybody else believes the canal should be built in Nicaragua. There are compelling reasons. Admiral Walker is still head of the Isthmian Canal Commission, but I understand he feels Nicaragua is the best route, too. So, there you are."

George nodded. "So, let's forget about the volcanoes and earthquakes in our path and start the Nicaraguan project?"

"Panama has one fatal flaw, too," said Roosevelt. "As we already discussed, the French still own the concession to build a canal there, and the only way we can get it from them is to pay an exorbitant fee for it."

"A fee of $109 million, I understand."

Roosevelt nodded vigorously. "You've been there. Do you think it's worth $109 million?"

"No, sir. Not even close. Mexico is still out of the running, I presume."

"Yes, George. Completely unfeasible. It would take a hundred years and the cost would bankrupt the nation—several times over."

"I suppose we *must* have this canal?"

"During the recent war with Spain, remember how long it took our ships to get from the Pacific to the Atlantic? Remember the *Oregon*? The war was over before it arrived." Roosevelt pounded his fist on his desk. "Yes, George. We *must* have this canal."

George was thinking. "If travel time is your reason for building it, Uncle Ted, then Panama should be the choice. The transit time through Panama would be a lot shorter. The Isthmus of Panama is the place, if only the French would come down on their price."

"Admiral Walker can't even get them to confirm the $109 million price. He's been trying for a year. It's impossible to deal with the French."

It seemed to George that the matter was settled. The canal would be in Nicaragua. He also noted that his uncle was becoming testy, so he'd better change the subject.

"Fine with me," said George. "I like Nicaragua and the Nicaraguans."

"That girl you killed the man over—Maria—she lives there, doesn't she? George, you're the worst fool I ever knew for getting into trouble with women. Damn it. Ever since Marion turned you down, you fall in love with a different one every day."

"Everybody has to have a hobby, Uncle." said George. Even though he'd met Maria only twice, he felt a bond with her.

Roosevelt roared. "Bully for you, I say. So, Nicaragua it's going to be! It'll give you a chance to go see that girl of yours if you want to. That is, of course, if you want to stay with the project. I want you to, you know. As long as I'm vice president, anyway."

"Thank you, sir. I've become damned interested in your canal. But," he added, not very convincingly, "I couldn't care less where you dig it."

The vice president drummed his fingers on his forehead. "There is only one person pushing for Panama. Only one. But he's making speeches and cornering everybody he can. He was the last chief of the *Compagnie*

Nouvelle du Canal de Panama, as they call it, before it went broke. He has Cromwell of Sullivan and Cromwell as his lawyer, and Cromwell has been helping him get around. But I think even Cromwell recognizes he's fighting for a lost cause and is getting discouraged. I don't remember the Frenchman's name, but I'll get it for you. I want you to go listen to what he has to say."

Roosevelt thumbed through a folder atop his desk. "I've got it," he said. "He's a fellow named Bunau-Varilla. He's been making friends. Senator Mark Hanna, for one; and even you must know he's influential as hell. I understand he's also working on President McKinley. Has some good arguments, writes a lot. Go catch one of his talks. He usually addresses pretty elite audiences, but I can get you in. Take notes. Report back and let me have your impressions."

So it was that young George Phillips sat spellbound as the distinguished-looking Frenchman addressed the New York Chamber of Commerce in fluent English. Bunau-Varilla was charismatic. He was dramatic and he was convincing. George carefully recorded his reasons for the U.S. building a canal in Panama:

1. A Panama Canal would be one-third the length of a Nicaraguan one.

2. It would have fewer curves, which would simplify the work.

3. It would cost less.

4. Panama, unlike Nicaragua, has no volcanoes.

5. Panama has had no earthquakes; Nicaragua has had many.

6. Panama has two good harbors.

7. Panama would require less excavation and fewer locks.

After the speech, George pushed through the crowd to speak to Bunau-Varilla. He was initially shunted aside by older, more important men. Finally, as the crowd began to thin out, George got his chance. "Excuse me, Monsieur Bunau-Varilla," he called. "I'm George Phillips, and I've been to Panama recently."

"Are you a newspaperman?" Bunau-Varilla asked hopefully.

"No, sir. I'm working for the vice president, Mr. Roosevelt."

"Happy to have you here," said Bunau-Varilla courteously. Then, with a smile and a wave, he turned to some men he considered more important.

Well, thought George, after you've already made friends with the president, why bother with the vice president.

That status would soon change. In September 1901, President McKinley was assassinated in Buffalo, New York. Theodore Roosevelt became the twenty-sixth president of the United States at the age of forty-two.

≈

Courtly, white haired John Tyler Morgan—senator from Alabama, former Confederate cavalry officer, and current chairman of the Senate Committee on Interoceanic Canals—received George Roosevelt Phillips, now an official aide to the president, into his office, courteously and formally. In government circles, Morgan was considered an authority on all canal matters. "I understand you've been in Central America, son," he said after the two had seated themselves.

"Yes, sir," said George.

"Your uncle sent you down to check on the Nicaraguan route, I suppose."

"Yes, sir."

"Are you now as convinced as I am that the canal should be built in Nicaragua?"

George nodded, more out of respect than conviction.

"The rest of the country feels the same way. I, sir, consider Panama to be a 'pesthole,' while Nicaragua is fertile and free of disease."

"I didn't know we were still really considering Panama, sir," said George.

"We're not. Besides, Nicaragua has sixty miles of navigable river and fifty miles of lake, both of which will cut down considerably on the amount of actual digging."

"Sir," said George, "the French have dug quite a bit on the Panama site, and they left a lot of equipment there, a lot of it usable."

"I have nothing but complete contempt for the French efforts to build a canal at Panama, and most Americans share my view," said Morgan. His words rang with scorn.

George had already been briefed that another reason for the senator's preference for Nicaragua was that a Nicaraguan canal would be closer to the southern U.S. Gulf, especially Mobile, Alabama. The Nicaraguan route would mean more money for his own, favored constituents.

"I'm very happy the matter has been decided, sir," said George. "And I congratulate you on your good work. I speak solely as a citizen, of course."

≈

George Phillips, in his new capacity as aide to the president, was warmly welcomed in Admiral Walker's office. On November 16, 1901, Walker's commission had recommended a Nicaraguan canal. Walker greeted him courteously and beckoned him to sit down in one of the cushioned leather chairs before him. George was amazed at the admiral's grasp of the situation and his expert knowledge. He realized he was talking to a man who knew more about the two canal routes than anybody he'd ever talked with. After Walker's lengthy analysis of the situation in both countries, George said boldly, "I've listened to every word you've said, sir; and the conclusion I draw is that Panama is the better route in practically all respects. Yet you still recommend Nicaragua. If I may ask, sir, why?"

Admiral Walker smiled. "Money."

"The French want too much for their holdings?"

The admiral nodded. "I've been trying for a year to get them to name a price. They won't give me one. That leaves us no alternative but to build in Nicaragua."

"In Panama somebody told me the French want $109 million."

"That's out of the question."

"Why won't they come right out and suggest a price?" asked George.

"They're French, and you know how the French are. If you have any doubts, ask Senator Morgan," the admiral chuckled.

George laughed. "Then Nicaragua it is."

≈

Walker's position was formally validated on November 21, 1901; and the Hearst newspapers published the findings of the Walker Commission recommending a Nicaraguan canal. Everybody agreed that this was the right decision.

George Phillips still brooded over Marion and what might have happened to her and her parents. The pain of lost love had subsided somewhat during the last few years, but she was still very much on his mind. He had received a letter from Larry telling him that Marion was dead, but the words didn't ring true. Larry took things like that more seriously. He wouldn't simply have said, "Marion died." When it counted, he was at heart a tender man, a gentleman first and last. He'd have expressed sympathy, told George how she had died, and how her family was taking it.

George had sold Beacon Hill. It was far too large for a single man, and the price he received for it helped him financially.

Now, in his New York townhouse on Madison Avenue, conveniently left to him by a great uncle, George was relaxing in his study, reading the recent newspaper articles regarding the future Nicaraguan canal. He did not fully grasp the engineering features. Tidal conditions. Locks to lift the ships in an elevator-like fashion. Although he'd heard some talk in Panama about locks, he had assumed they were to control the tides at the Pacific end of the canal.

His musings were interrupted by his manservant. More than a houseboy, less than a butler, Coleman had served the townhouse's previous residents for thirty years and stayed on to work for George when he moved into the house. "A gentleman is waiting for you in the living room, sir," Coleman announced.

Pulling on his coat and straightening his necktie, George asked, "Who is it? Anybody I know?"

Coleman shrugged. "I have never seen him before, sir."

Standing in the living room, admiring a painting, was Bunau-Varilla. Surprised, Phillips strode toward the well-dressed and immaculately groomed little Frenchman. George smiled and put his hand out to shake Bunau-Varilla's.

After their mutual greetings, George said politely, "And what can I do for you, monsieur? Would you like a brandy? Some coffee or tea, perhaps?"

Bunau-Varilla shook his head vigorously. "No, sir," he said, bowing from the waist. "First, I want to apologize for not being able to spend more time with you after my speech at the Chamber of Commerce."

"Oh, no offense was taken," said George, waving his right hand airily. "After all, I'm just a young man."

The Frenchman bowed again. "You are the nephew of the president of the United States," he said. "I treated you shabbily."

"Oh," said George. "It's all water over the dam now, anyway. You know, of course, that the canal will be built in Nicaragua."

"Yes. For us, the situation is as bad as it possibly could be. I seem to be the only advocate for a canal through Panama. I stand alone, without allies, without supporters, without anything but hope."

"I don't think I can help you," said George. "Everybody's mind is made up. With all respect, sir, the canal will be built in Nicaragua."

Philippe Bunau-Varilla looked dejected and had to visibly steady himself before continuing. After a pause, the Frenchman cleared his throat and continued, "Monsieur Phillips, I have gone over all the reports of the American committees. There is only one reason you have chosen Nicaragua over Panama."

George thought for a minute and said, "Yes, you're right. The only reason for not choosing Panama—aside from the fact that Senator Morgan favors Nicaragua—is that you and your French company want too much money for too few assets."

"How do you know how much we want?" asked Bunau-Varilla.

"Everybody says you want $109 million."

"Ah," replied the Frenchman. "But tell me, Monsieur Phillips, have we ever officially quoted that figure to your people?"

"No," snapped George, his tone sharper than before. "You haven't ever answered any of our requests for a price. So, because of your lack of response, we made another choice."

The Frenchman eyed George craftily. He smiled. "What would you consider a fair price?" he asked. "A price that would cause the Walker Commission to reconsider its recommendation?"

George was plainly taken aback, momentarily losing his edge. "How should I know?"

"I have attempted to talk to your uncle, Monsieur Phillips, without achieving any success. This evening I depart for France. I must put in order the house of the *Compagnie Nouvelle*. Perhaps you will do for me a favor?"

"It all depends. What kind of a favor?"

"Find out from Admiral Walker and from your uncle the highest price they are willing to pay for our concessions and equipment and cable the figure to me in Paris."

George tried to hide his excitement as he motioned for Bunau-Varilla to sit down in one of the comfortable chairs. Would this be a treasonable act, he wondered. No. It could actually benefit his country. He also wondered if Admiral Walker and the president had a figure in mind. If not, how fast could they come up with one? It was worth a try.

"I'll do the best I can," said George, finally. "No promises, though. Just give me your cable address in Paris."

Two weeks later, on December 2, 1901, Phillips stood in the Oval Office with the president and Admiral Walker. He had requested the urgent meeting and had just asked them what value they had put on the *Compagnie Nouvelle*'s Panama assets.

"You've seen their stuff, George," said the president. "What's it worth?"

"I'd much prefer to hear what Admiral Walker thinks," said George.

"Theodore, you are a rascal," said the admiral. "We've all come up with the same figure, and you know it." He turned to Phillips. "A price of $40 million for everything. And that includes the railroad."

"I'd say that's a bargain, sir," said George.

"It's the most we can pay and still be able to convince Congress to vote for the Panama route."

"Can I unofficially, as a private citizen, advise the French of your offer?" asked George.

"Certainly," replied the president. "It can do no harm and will tell us where we stand."

Time was working against Panama. On December 4, 1901, there was still no firm offer by the French, and the Canal Commission Report recommended Nicaragua to Congress. The Nicaraguan plan was approved. Only six days later, with little pomp and ceremony, a formal diplomatic convention was signed in Managua "with a view to the construction of a Nicaraguan Canal by the United States."

Immediately following his meeting with the president, George Phillips had sent the following cable: VARILLA PARIS: FORTY MILLION DOLLARS TOPS. REGARDS, GEORGE. He had received no response. He agonized over having sent it. Did he do the right thing? The president had given his permission, so why worry? He woke up at two a.m. His brain seemed to work better in the wee hours of the night. If the money problem could be solved by paying the French forty million dollars, then the Panama project could go ahead, to the benefit of the United States. He had *not* betrayed his country. He had benefited it by giving it an alternate location for his uncle's canal. Now, if the damned Frenchman ever answered his cable, the United States would be free to build a canal in Panama or in Nicaragua, whichever it chose. What was taking so long?

In France, after much lobbying, Bunau-Varilla had finally been able to convince shareholders to consider the smaller offer. He knew his timing was crucial. He had to act quickly. Little did he know that on January 8, 1902, the U.S. House of Representatives authorized a Nicaraguan canal after only two days of debate.

The very next day, the Walker Commission received the following cable from Paris: OFFER TURN OVER TO YOU ALL ASSETS FRENCH CANAL COMPANY IN PANAMA FOR TOTAL SUM FORTY MILLION DOLLARS.

Roosevelt summoned Senator Morgan to his office on January 16, 1902, to discuss the most recent development. Morgan was first elected to the Senate of the United States from Alabama in 1876, which made him a senior senator, one with influence and experience. He was adamant. He wanted the Nicaraguan site. The matter was closed as far as he was concerned. Again he called Panama a pesthole, the Frenchmen crooks. He described Nicaragua as an earthly paradise. Strong-minded, outspoken, and inflexible, Senator Morgan was highly intelligent and unabashedly patriotic, notwithstanding his service in the Confederate cavalry. In fact, Morgan was probably one of the most respected men in the U.S. Senate.

≈

On January 18, 1902, the Walker Commission reversed itself. It recommended to President Roosevelt the building of a lock-type canal in Panama.

≈

Admiral Walker stated that the only reason they had not chosen Panama initially was because of the high price the French had put on their holdings there. The new price was acceptable, and all other considerations were favorable to building the canal in Panama.

On February 7, hearings began again. Walker appeared before the Morgan Committee. Admiral Walker and Senator Morgan were good friends. Although both retained their dignity in the controversy over the two routes, their difference of opinion was quite visible. Morgan and his committee were not receptive to Walker's arguments. Hearings continued through March. The Morgan Committee voted seven to four in favor of a Nicaraguan canal. The odds against Panama being chosen by the Senate as the site for the canal were now about a hundred to one. Glossed over in every debate, however, was the fact that Nicaragua had what George Phillips had described as "that one fatal flaw."

Never mentioned were "seismic disturbances." Earthquakes and volcanoes had been pretty much dismissed as not being serious threats to a canal in either Nicaragua or Panama.

In his uncle's study, George sat discussing the events of the past two months with the president. Both men were relaxed. "I'm not going back to Nicaragua," said George.

"Oh?" said Roosevelt. "You're a bad loser, George." The president smiled his toothy grin.

George smiled back. "No, my dear uncle. I'm afraid of earthquakes. A bad one can kill thousands. And do you know, Mr. President, nobody, not one, even mentioned the fact that Nicaragua has earthquakes every few years, and that Panama has yet to experience its first one?"

"You're angry, George. I know. Whenever you call me 'Mr. President,' you're mad as hell."

"Disappointed," said George. "We're acting like a bunch of ostriches, sticking our heads in the sand."

The president reflected. "It's not completely over yet, George. Maybe this will be the year they'll have an earthquake." He grinned and reached for his cigar. He was joking, of course.

CHAPTER

But nature has a way of encroaching on man's best laid plans. On May 8, 1902 Mount Pelée on Martinique erupted, wiping out the city of St. Pierre and killing at least 30,000 people. It erupted again twelve days later. Prompted to inquire about the same possibilities in Nicaragua, Senator Morgan had sent a cabled inquiry to President Zelaya of Nicaragua, who responded through his representative in Washington that recent reports of similar volcanic eruptions and earthquakes in Nicaragua were "entirely false."

On June 4, 1902, the U.S. Senate resumed its debate on the proposed canal site. Senator Morgan was still firmly in favor of Nicaragua, even though President Zelaya's disclaimer had been exposed as an outright lie by George Phillips after he had checked with his Nicaraguan contacts. The press reports confirmed him. Momotombo had blown. But Nicaragua continued to deny it.

Philippe Bunau-Varilla gave his personal staff a challenge: to purchase every one-penny Nicaraguan postage stamp they could find. On the stamp was the picture of the volcano, Momotombo, spewing smoke. Bunau-Varilla managed to obtain enough of these Nicaraguan stamps to attach one to a piece of paper placed on the desk of each of the ninety

U.S. Senators. Whether these stamps made a difference was unclear, but most people felt they definitely had some influence.

As the hotly contested debates continued, George assisted his uncle in matters of state. He was anxious to see the canal matter resolved. Perhaps his uncle realized that George's first "assignment" to Nicaragua would whet his appetite for political adventure.

On June 5, 1902, following Bunau-Varilla's ingenious ploy with the stamps, Senator Mark Hanna spoke on the Senate floor advocating that the canal be built in Panama. He proclaimed, "All engineering and practical questions involved in the construction of a Panama Canal are satisfactorily settled and assured." Two weeks later the Senate passed the Panama Canal bill by a vote of forty-two to thirty-four. It was close. If only five more senators had voted for Nicaragua against Panama, the Nicaraguan route would have been chosen.

On June 26, the U.S. House of Representatives passed the Panama Canal bill. Considering his growing apprehension about the seismic activity in Nicaragua, George felt relieved. The right decision had been made.

On a warm afternoon, George strolled aimlessly along the Potomac River. Stopping for a rest under a cherry tree, he crouched on a grassy patch, wiped his brow with a handkerchief, and perused his newspaper. As his uncle's aide-de-camp, there had been precious little time for leisure activity in the previous year as he closely monitored the chaotic developments in the Panama–Nicaragua debates.

George reflected on the mass of political activity that had transpired. Everything had progressed smoothly enough, up to a point. On March 17, 1903, the treaty signed by Secretary of State John Hay and Colombia's chargé d'affaires in Washington, Thomas Herrán, known as the Hay-Herrán Treaty, was ratified by the United States Senate. Three months earlier, on January 22, 1903, it had been duly signed by the United States and Colombia. Under the terms of this treaty, Colombia granted the U.S. the concession to build a canal from the Atlantic to the Pacific through the Isthmus of Panama. Colombia also granted the U.S. control of a Canal Zone six miles wide, three miles on each side of the canal, for *operational* purposes. In return, the United States would pay a lump sum of $10 million to Colombia and $250,000 per year thereafter. The treaty would be renegotiated after one hundred years, at the option of the United States.

This treaty was about the same as the one previously proposed with Nicaragua.

The matter wasn't closed yet, George remembered. The Colombian Senate, supported by strong public opinion, felt that the document was far too favorable to the United States and detrimental to Colombia. They wanted the right to negotiate their own settlement with the French company, *Compagnie Nouvelle.* They felt the proposed $250,000 annual payment by the U.S. was far too small, particularly in light of the fact that it was the same amount already being paid by the Panama Railroad, a much smaller and less significant enterprise already included in the French assets obtained by the U.S. Additionally, Colombian sovereignty over the Canal Zone was not clearly defined, although it was supposedly granted by the treaty; and Colombia felt they deserved another $10 million payment, to come from the French company's $40 million, which the U.S. refused.

At the time, George had to agree that the Colombian contentions were, indeed, all valid. Had the U.S. been a little more generous, flexible and tactful, allowing Colombia to negotiate its own agreement with the *Compagnie Nouvelle,* as it was legally entitled to do, everything might have turned out to everybody's benefit. Instead, the U.S. legislators accused Colombians of being bandits who were trying to hold up the U.S. at gunpoint. This was far from the case. Until 1903, as someone noted, the U.S. had no better friend south of the Rio Grande than Colombia. This friendship was a direct legacy of Simón Bolívar, the great South American liberator, who practically worshipped George Washington and whose regard for the political ideals of the United States was enormous. The Great Liberator had actually modeled the Colombian federal and state system on that of the United States.

After the rejection by the Colombian Congress, a rejection that so easily could have been averted, a few of the top men in the U.S. government began to think they should open negotiations with Nicaragua again. That would be swift, uncomplicated, and easy. Instead, the U.S. backed the Panamanian separatists in their revolution of November 1903. This was a serious, patriotic revolution as far as Panama was concerned. Prominent people had pledged their lives, their fortunes, and their sacred honor in the cause of freedom from an unsympathetic Colombian government. As it happened, the actual insurrection became more of a comic opera than a bloody revolution.

"We watched the Colombian fleet sail ominously into our harbor," George's friend, Juan de la Guardia, wrote from Panama City. "They demanded our surrender and threatened to bombard the city if we did not capitulate by dawn. We patriots responded with a firm, 'We shall never surrender!' We were fearful, but resolute, my friend.

"Much to our surprise the Colombian battleship fired only one shell, killing a poor Chinese laundryman on his way to work. We learned later that that one shell was the only one on board and that the other warships were unarmed! Can you imagine, it was all bluster. The Colombian admiral gave orders to steam home—after that one shot!

"So much for the 'bombardment' of Panama, George. We are all safe and we await your visit to our new country," Juan concluded happily.

On the Atlantic side of the Isthmus, George discovered, the Colombian Army landed. Its general marched to the offices of the Panama Railroad and demanded transportation to Panama City. "Certainly, sir," said the station clerk. "How many men do you have, sir?"

"Two thousand," said the general.

"Well, at five dollars per head, that will be ten thousand dollars," said the clerk.

"No, no," said the general. "Read your contract. The Colombian Army travels free on this railroad. It is part of your concession." He stormed out of the clerk's office.

For the next three days, the general showed up at the railroad office every morning. And every morning the clerk told him he was still searching through the concession document. But the text of the concession was very long, and he was having a hard time finding the particular clause.

Finally, the clerk, hanging his head in shame, said he had, indeed, found the clause and the Colombian Army was entitled to free passage on the railroad. To make up for his error, he offered the general and his staff the special railroad car usually reserved for the president of the railroad. They were flattered, accepted the offer, and were quickly on their way to Panama City—where they were met by several battalions of Panamanian soldiers and patriotic sympathizers who escorted the Colombians to jail. Their army was still in the dock city of Colon, since all the passenger cars of the railroad had been safely sent to Panama City, and there was no other transportation available.

At that point, warships with names like *Dixie, Atlanta, Maine, Mayflower,* and *Prairie* anchored off Colon on the Atlantic, and others named *Boston, Marblehead, Concord,* and *Wyoming* steamed into Panama Bay. By their mere presence, Panama's independence was now assured. On November 6, 1903, the U.S. officially recognized the Republic of Panama.

≈

Naturally, the secession of Panama from Colombia caused a great deal of controversy in the United States. The press was divided. One U.S senator writing in an influential magazine said, "We did our duty. If the people of

Panama had not revolted, I should have recommended to Congress to take possession of the Isthmus by force." Negative commentary was just as strong. Editorial cartoons depicted Roosevelt as a big bully usurping imperialistic expansion by means of gunboat diplomacy.

The pros and cons of the U.S. action in Panama were hotly debated. To adverse criticism from many quarters, Roosevelt energetically responded, "To submit my actions for approval of the Congress would have consumed at least fifty years. So I acted. I *took* Panama. Now you can debate to your heart's content!"

Still, Roosevelt resented the attacks on him and asked the Attorney General, Philander Knox, to construct his defense. Knox's comment was, "Oh, Mr. President, please do not let so great an achievement suffer from any taint of legality."

On another occasion, at a cabinet meeting, Roosevelt delivered a long speech defending his position on Panama. "Have I made myself clear?" he asked at the end of it. "Have I answered the charges?"

Elihu Root, cabinet member and a famous wit, replied, "You certainly have, Mr. President. You were accused of seduction and you have conclusively proved that you were guilty of rape!"

≈

George Phillips kept his opinions to himself but thought the matter had been handled poorly. Still, he had to defend his uncle, the president. "We are not a patient people," he proclaimed in private, remembering the phrase. "We thought we had a treaty with Colombia and they double-crossed us. Turned us down cold. What do you want us to do? Say, 'Yes, sir,' to Colombia and forget about building a canal?"

"Ever consider negotiating with Colombia?" asked one of his friends.

"We already had, remember? That's when we made the treaty."

"George, was it a fair treaty? Did we give them a square deal?"

George simply shook his head. Then, he said, "No. It wasn't. But it was a done deal. Both countries agreed to it. But you're right. We should have let the Colombians negotiate directly with the *Compagnie Nouvelle*, then made our treaty. But it would have taken too much time, so we just separated Panama from Colombia."

George always felt better after telling the truth. He felt better now.

Philippe Bunau-Varilla considered himself the savior of Panama and the primary force behind the canal being built in Panamanian territory. He pressured Manuel Amador Guerrero, the head of the new republic, to name him Panama's ambassador to the United States with full diplomatic powers until a permanent representative could be appointed. Amador initially balked at the idea, certain that the Panamanian people would object to a foreigner assuming that role. But convinced that Bunau-Varilla would be an asset in getting the treaty signed, he conceded. He told Bunau-Varilla specifically not to negotiate a canal treaty, since he, Carlos Arosemena, and Federico Boyd were already on their way to Washington for this purpose. All three were signers of Panama's Declaration of Independence and were true patriots working for the benefit of their new nation.

≈

George Phillips, still his uncle's aide-de-camp, had mixed emotions. The politics surrounding the issue were mind-boggling. He understood Panama's desire to have the canal built within its territory, but he also understood Colombia's reasons for rejecting the Hay-Herrán Treaty. Anyway, he thought, the Panamanian delegation will be here soon and everything will be settled.

He liked chatting with John Hay, the secretary of state, with whom he had developed a friendship outside the office. He had learned a lot from that gentleman. On the evening of November 18, he decided to drop by Mr. Hay's home for a chat and, perhaps, an invitation to dinner. "The secretary has been very busy today," his servant told George as he escorted him into the front hall, "but I'm sure he will see you, sir." George liked Hay, a big man with a giant, walrus moustache and an incongruously mild disposition. He was always courteous, and had an extremely quick mind and a wry sense of humor.

Hay was seated in his study, a small former drawing room with blue walls overlooking Lafayette Square. From there, he could see the lights of the White House. Rising, Hay held out his hand to George. "You just missed your French friend," said Hay. "He just left."

"You mean Monsieur Bunau-Varilla?"

"The very one. Nice chap. Extremely nice. We both signed the treaty about seven this very evening."

"You did?" George was surprised. He knew a Panamanian delegation was on its way to Washington to discuss terms and would arrive that very evening. "You did?" he repeated, incredulous.

"Aren't you pleased? The treaty is signed. And you are acquainted with Bunau-Varilla. I've seen you with him."

"Yes," said George, slowly. "Be careful of him. He's out for himself."

"He's also Panama's ambassador to the United States and has full ambassadorial powers," countered Hay.

George was silent. "He's *ad interim* until a proper ambassador can be appointed. I don't believe he's empowered to do very much. I certainly do not believe he is empowered to sign the Panama Canal Treaty!"

"There's nothing in his appointment—and I've gone over it carefully—that prohibits him from doing anything any other ambassador can do."

"What is all this supposed to mean?" George asked with much trepidation.

Hay smiled. "Monsieur Bunau-Varilla wanted a treaty so badly he could taste it. Wanted *his* name on it. So he granted us a lot more than we ever asked for."

"What? I don't believe it. And I'm not sure I like it."

"It's like the other canal treaties, pretty much, except...." Hay paused mid-sentence to grab a folder off of his desk. He found the notes he was looking for and continued, "Panama grants the United States the right not only to build and operate a canal connecting the Atlantic and Pacific Oceans, but, *in perpetuity*, the use, occupation, and control of a Canal Zone, approximately ten miles wide, over which the United States will possess *full sovereign rights to the entire exclusion of the exercise by the Republic of Panama of any such sovereign rights, power, or authority.*"

"In perpetuity means *forever*. What do we give?" asked George.

"Oh, the usual $10 million plus $250,000 per year. And we guarantee the independence of the Republic of Panama."

"Why, Mr. Hay, that's highway robbery. It's grotesque. You turned him down, of course."

Hay looked at his young friend and smiled. "George, my friend, you still have a lot to learn. When you get an offer as good as this, take it and run."

Both men were silent for a few minutes. Then George said, "This will cause trouble, you know. The Panamanians love us now, but they'll hate us as soon as they find out what we've done to them. You negotiated this thing with Bunau-Varilla? He's an adventurer, an opportunist."

"George, if it hadn't been for him, we wouldn't be building a canal in Panama at all. If it hadn't been for him, there would not *be* a Republic of Panama."

George smiled wryly. "He's like Benedict Arnold," he said. "The hero of Saratoga and the traitor of West Point."

"It's over," said Hay.

"I'd hate to be at the railroad station with Bunau-Varilla when he tells Arosemena, Boyd, and Amador what he's just done," George snapped.

Secretary of State John Hay nodded his head. "So would I."

≈

They were right. There was pandemonium at Union Station when the official treaty negotiators were told by Bunau-Varilla that he had already signed a treaty, and they could have saved themselves a trip. But that was nothing compared to their outrage when they arrived at their hotel and read the actual terms.

"*Sovereignty!*" screamed Amador.

"*In perpetuity!*" shouted Boyd.

"*To the exclusion of the exercise of our rights in our own country!*" said Arosemena in astonishment. Bunau-Varilla was lucky to get out of the hotel room alive.

On February 23, 1904, the U.S. Senate ratified the Hay–Bunau-Varilla Treaty by a vote of sixty-six to fourteen, transferring the title of the canal from the French to the United States, and granting the U.S. occupation, use, and control of the ten-mile strip of land surrounding the canal.

The Panamanian delegation, naturally, objected to what they considered the most intolerable clauses of the treaty, insisting that all terms be the same as they were negotiated for the Hay-Herrán and Nicaraguan treaties. This was what had been agreed before the delegation left Panama. In a meeting in the Oval Office, at which George was present, both President Roosevelt and Secretary Hay cautioned the legitimate Panamanian government representatives that their government should not oppose the Hay–Bunau-Varilla Treaty. "You know," said Hay, "the Colombian government has offered to accept the same treaty you are resisting if we'll agree to help them re-annex Panama to Colombia."

"And won't you look like fools if that happens," said Boyd. "You'll be the laughingstock of South America. Nobody will ever trust or respect you again."

"There are other ways to handle the situation," said the president.

Even Secretary Hay appeared shocked by Roosevelt's thinly veiled threat to simply annex Panama as a territory if they did not accept the treaty.

"You're implying you could take over Panama if we don't ratify your treaty. That's what you mean, isn't it? Well, you cannot do that," said Federico Boyd. "We're too far away."

"We annexed Hawaii," said Hay. "That's farther away than Panama."

"In all fairness, sir, this treaty was drawn between a Frenchman and an American. No Panamanians were even consulted," commented Manuel Amador.

"Bunau-Varilla was your representative," said Hay. "His credentials were in order."

"Besides," said President Roosevelt, "the articles to which you refer were proposed by *your* representative, *not* by Mr. Hay."

"That's right," said Hay. "We simply *accepted* the terms proposed by your emissary."

He had them. Panama was trapped into an agreement it did not want but could not get out of. The Hay–Bunau-Varilla Treaty was an accomplished fact. Newborn, Panama had already been betrayed.

George Phillips was disgusted with Bunau-Varilla. The so-called diplomat had been motivated by sheer ego, he thought. His actions had been based solely on his desire to have the canal treaty bear *his* name, and for the money he'd get from *Compagnie Nouvelle*. It was a selfish, self-centered move. Before Bunau-Varilla departed for France, George called on him at his hotel in New York. After a perfunctory, "Good morning," George lashed out. "I never should have sent you that cablegram! We should have let things stand as they were and built a canal in Nicaragua. You, sir, have sown a bad seed that will sprout a poisoned weed. There was no need for this, sir! None!"

"Do not be so passionate, my young friend. Panama is now a country, free from Colombia. Panama will have a canal that will provide economic security beyond its most cherished dreams. I made the offer for the good of the country. To ensure the canal would be built there. I nailed it down, as you Americans say."

"It was already nailed down!" shouted George. "You didn't have to give away the store."

"I did what I thought best for Panama."

"You did what you thought best for Philippe Bunau-Varilla."

"Good day to you, sir." The Frenchman bowed and turned his back on his guest.

George had no alternative but to leave, knowing that no action was possible at this point.

Worn out from seemingly fruitless negotiations, George requested time off from his position. Roosevelt concurred. The two had been at odds over the Panama question, and it was best for George to get away for awhile. They both agreed to leave things open. If the president required George's services, he would return to government. If there was no reason to return, he did not have to.

He came into the White House the following morning and began to clean out his desk. One of George's young friends, who was an assistant to a senator from Texas, poked his curly, brown head around the door. "A gentleman to see you, George. You receiving? He has two beautiful young ladies with him."

George smiled and tossed a law book at his friend. "Of course, I'm receiving, you mutt," he said. "Show the ladies in, for Pete's sake."

"I don't know," said the Texan. "They're pretty important constituents of my boss."

Soon, smiling from ear to ear, Larry Kingman, George's old Rough Riders pal, strode through the door. In his wake were two striking young ladies. George threw his arms around Larry in a warm *abrazo*, a habit he'd picked up in Latin America. "Gosh! I sure am glad to see you," he said, beaming.

"How are you, old man?" said Larry just as cordially. "I want you to meet my wife. George, this is Julie."

Julie Kingman was a tall, pretty brunette with an upturned nose and lovely curving lips. Her dark brown eyes sparkled. Shaking her hand vigorously, George said, "I couldn't be more delighted. Larry's a very lucky man!"

"And this is my sister, Sophie Wentworth," continued Larry, waving his hand toward the other lady. George turned his attention to Sophie. She was the most lovely girl he had ever seen. Her golden blonde hair set off a sun-tanned face with gracefully chiseled features. Her figure was flawless, if a little on the slim side. Except where it counts, George thought.

He bowed gracefully. "Enchanted," he said. And he really was. Then, unexpectedly, even for him, he asked, "And where is Mr. Wentworth?"

Answering for his sister, Larry said, "Sophie's a widow. She was married to Tom Wentworth who owned the spread next to ours, but he was killed in an accident right after they were married."

"I'm terribly sorry," began George.

Sophie cut in. "He was a drunk and shot it out with another drunk in a saloon one night."

"Sophie!" said Larry, embarrassed by her frankness.

A little taken aback by the Texans' manner, George decided to change the subject. "Listen, how about the four of us having dinner tonight? I'll come by for you. Where are you staying?"

"We accept, and we're at the old Willard," said Larry. George was learning that men made the decisions about such things in Texas.

CHAPTER

George took the Kingman party to the best restaurant he knew in Washington, the Occidental. After seating Julie Kingman on his right, Sophie on his left, and Larry opposite him, George made small talk for a few minutes. Then, he took the plunge and said, "Larry, you wrote me that Marion was dead. What happened? And what about the rest of the family? Actually, old friend, you told me nothing."

"I'm sorry, George. It's a sad tale. Mr. Wendell was a teller in a bank in Fort Worth. Got himself shot and killed in the last hold-up we had. When the bank robbers came in, he ran out of his teller's cage shooting this little pop-gun of a pistol. They cut him down so fast he was dead before he hit the floor. Scared them off, though. They left the way they came in, without grabbing a nickel. The bank was talking about putting up a statue to Wendell, except there was no place to put it. Stockyards got in the way. Then the new packing plant. The town's been cleaned up since then, safe as houses now."

George asked, "What happened to his family? Mrs. Wendell and Marion?"

"Well, George, Mrs. Wendell married the richest bachelor in town and went to live on his ranch. I hear they're very happy. Mr. Wendell, as you well know, was a hard, difficult man. Ordered his wife around like a ranchhand. So, she's much better off if you ask me."

"And Marion?" George's heart thumped as he asked the question again, impatient with Larry's slow delivery.

"Marion was a very pretty girl. She caught the eye of a man named Six Gun Smith. A handsome man. All the ladies loved him. And we men. We liked old Six Gun. He was one of the last of the old breed. About fifty years old, he rode with most of the gunslingers in the 80's, late 70's, too, I bet. Had scars from gunfights all over him, they say. Well, little Miss Wendell, she fell hard for old Six Gun, and nobody can blame her for that. But we were still surprised when she left home and rode off with him."

George tried to hide his disbelief. "Rode off with him? That doesn't sound at all like the Marion I knew. Where are they now?"

Larry shook his head slowly. "It's a long story, George."

"We have all evening."

Larry frowned and appeared embarrassed. "How do you want this, George? Straight? Or full of sugar syrup?"

"You know me, Larry. What do you think?"

"Well, here goes. Like I said, your friend Marion ran off with old Six Gun. Then there was a series of bank robberies, way out in west Texas. It seems the Smiths had been gathering up a grub stake to buy a ranch that was for sale. The trouble was, the previous owner didn't include the stock, so they'd spent all their money on a ranch with nothing on it. Times are good, and you can get away with that sort of thing."

"I don't think they ever actually got married," added Julie tentatively.

"Just like a woman to bring up something like that," said Larry to George. "That has nothing to do with it, honey. Fact is, other ranchers' herds began coming up short. Horses started going missing, too. A bunch went over to Smith's, but he'd fixed the brands so well nobody could say for sure they were theirs. But they knew. A man who runs cattle like I do gets to know his herd. You can just plain tell that those steers or heifers are yours by the way they walk or eat and everything. You raised the critters, by damn, and if you can't pick out your own, there's something wrong with you.

So, the people living around that part of the state got together and started setting up ambushes for rustlers. We call them *posses*. Duly deputized by the marshal and all that. But they came up dry, month after month. Started to figure the Smiths had all the stock they needed and wouldn't be taking any more of theirs. So they set one last trap at a horse ranch that hadn't been hit; and do you know, two riders came loping in just as easy as you please and started cutting out a bunch of good horses and driving them right off the ranch. It all happened so fast, the posse almost didn't see them ride out with the mounts. It took them a good fifteen minutes to catch up with the pair, then they yelled, 'Stop! Stop or we'll shoot!' But the horse thieves rode faster until they made one mistake. They abandoned the stolen horses, which were giving them some cover from the posse. When they went galloping off alone, they made too good a target in moonlight.

Larry paused and reached his hand out toward his friend. "I'm sorry, George, but Marion was shot dead along with Six Gun. But I gotta admit, the posse treated the bodies with respect. Didn't drag them into town by their heels or anything like that. Waited until morning, and sent out a flatbed with two horses and brought them in real gentle. Gave them a good burial, too. You see, George, everybody really liked old Six Gun, even though he had a bandit's heart in him. And Marion was a lady. Yes. They treated them real good. Buried them well, too."

George's eyes were moist. But he got his grief under control quickly. "You wouldn't be pouring a little sugar syrup now, would you, Larry?"

"Not a lot," said Larry. "That was pretty much how it happened."

"Marion was out of her element," commented George. "She was an Easterner. I hadn't realized how badly her father treated his family."

George guessed what had really happened. Mr. Wendell had had enough of this world. Standing up to the bank robbers was the easy way out. He guessed that Wendell simply had one more tragedy than he could handle. That was probably the reason he rode his wife and daughter so hard, until Marion just *had* to get away. That was why she'd run off with Six Gun Smith. What a shame. Wendell had gone from being a prosperous Boston banker to being a clerk in a small-town bank. And, being an arrogant, pompous man, he couldn't have been liked there. No friends. No future.

CHAPTER

It was obvious that Julie Kingman felt comfortable with her husband's friend. "I feel I've known you a long time, George Phillips," she said. "Larry talks about you constantly. What have you been doing lately, George? Something pretty exciting, I bet."

"No, Julie—I mean, yes, Julie."

They all laughed. Julie had broken the log-jam in George's brain.

Smiling now, George said, "Well, first I went back and graduated from Harvard. After that, I went to Washington to talk to my uncle, who was only vice president then. And, do you know what? He sent me to Nicaragua, and I ended up in Panama."

"Ooh!" exclaimed Sophie. "The Panama Canal!"

"Well, there's no canal there yet. They haven't started to dig."

"But you were *there!* Oh, George! You have to tell us all about it."

"Now!" said Julie. "Tell us all about Panama and that other place you mentioned. Tell us about the president."

"I want to meet the president," said Sophie.

"You will," said George.

"What do you think about this Panama thing?" asked Julie.

"Well, Julie, Sophie, both Panama and Nicaragua are sort of like Texas. You'd feel more at home in Nicaragua. Good cattle country, but so is Panama in some places." George put his fingers to his forehead, which he often did when he was thinking. "You see, all the politicians were having a hard time deciding whether to dig the canal in Nicaragua or in Panama, and I got in the middle of it, got made a fool of by a clever Frenchman."

"Do you hear that, Larry, honey? George was right in the middle of all the excitement."

"I wish I hadn't been. It was a long haul and the whole thing just turns my stomach at this point. I can't tell you how good it is to be here with you, just relaxing."

George's woeful expression had a sobering effect on the Kingmans. "Why don't you visit us in Texas, George?" said Larry. "There aren't any spreads for sale right now that I know of, but something might come up. I bet you could trade in those shoes for some proper boots!"

"Maybe I'll just do that!" George sounded serious, despite Larry's tongue-in-cheek invitation. He could imagine telling Coleman to take good care of the house on Madison Avenue and hanging a sign on his door saying, "GONE TO TEXAS." He remembered that's what people did in the old days. It made him smile. But this was 1904, thought George.

As crazy as it seemed, George knew he'd fallen hopelessly in love with Sophie the minute he saw her and she had said, "I am so very pleased to meet you, George. You've been my hero ever since I heard from Larry what wonderful, brave things you did in Cuba."

After finishing dinner, both men lit cigars and relaxed in their chairs. "How long will you be here?" asked George, suddenly realizing why he was interested in the answer.

Larry smiled. "As long as we want to. I decided you were the first friend I wanted to visit."

"And both Sophie and I wanted so badly to meet you," said Julie.

George scratched his head. "I honestly couldn't be happier to see anybody in my life," he said. "But why now? Something's happened. I can tell by your voices."

"Oh," said Sophie feigning casualness, "we've discovered oil on our properties, both Larry's and mine." She smiled like a cat who had just swallowed a canary. "So, we are now free to do whatever we want to do."

"What do you want to do?" asked George earnestly.

Sophie shrugged.

"She hates Texas and wants to stay in the East," said Julie. "She wants to be a lady."

"She *is* a lady," George objected.

"Well," said Julie, "if riding a horse, roping calves, barbecuing a steer, and driving cattle make you a lady, I guess you're right!"

"I'm impressed," said George.

Her elbow on the table, Sophie leaned forward and rested her chin in her palm. "I knew I'd like you, George."

Larry raised his eyebrows. "It's getting late."

"When can we meet the president?" asked Sophie.

"Larry is one of my uncle's favorite people. Let me see if I can set it up for tomorrow sometime," said George.

≈

The meeting with President Roosevelt went beautifully, as George knew it would. As they left his office, George could overhear Sophie whispering to Larry, "Just think, Larry, George is a nephew of the president! Wow! He's a real gentleman, isn't he, Larry? So cultured, so educated and easy to talk to, so distinguished. Do you think he likes me, Bubba?"

"He won't if he hears you call me 'Bubba'."

"Oh, Larry. I think he likes me. Do you think he does?"

"George likes almost everybody," said Larry truthfully.

"Oh, you know what I mean. Does he *like* me?"

George caught up with the Kingmans. "Now you've met the president of the United States. What do you think of him?"

They all answered at the same time, so George couldn't make out a word they said, but he gathered they thought very highly of the president.

≈

At lunch after their meeting with Roosevelt, George asked with concern, "Tell me, Larry, what are your plans now?"

"Well, we thought we'd go to Europe," said Larry. "First to New York, of course. I've always wanted to see the big city."

George's eyes lit up. "Your arrival must be fate, Larry. I'm leaving Washington. I was about to pack up when you and your family arrived. I have a townhouse in New York, and that's where I'm headed. I'm afraid it's too small to accommodate you, though."

"We have reservations at the Waldorf Astoria Hotel on Fifth Avenue. Two suites, one for Julie and me and one for Sophie."

George smiled. "Great," he said happily. "Then I'll be able to show you New York."

Larry put his arm around his friend and whispered in his ear. "You and Sophie seem to hit it off real good. She'd really like to see New York, especially with you."

21

Glad to be back in his own home, George arranged a dinner party for the Kingman clan to introduce them to some New Yorkers. The polished city-dwellers weren't used to the Texans' way of talking. They looked mystified at such expressions as "hornswoggled" and "prickly as a young cactus" or "He took off like a cat on fire." George discovered that Texans were used to dining in their kitchens using simple steel knives, forks, and spoons, and were ill-at-ease with his precious silver and the number of utensils set before them.

Afterward, the Kingmans stayed for a few minutes. "We don't fit in here, do we, George?" said Larry.

George had been reluctantly thinking the same thing. "Larry," he said, "New Yorkers and Texans are different from each other. Neither is better nor inferior than the other. They're just different. For example, if I were to go to Texas and talk the way I do and expect things to be like they are here, people would think me strange. They'd make fun of me, right?"

"Are people here laughing at us, George?"

George shook his head. "No, not yet. You are a novel experience for New York society. I think they enjoyed you tremendously. You're different, you're a new sensation. New Yorkers like that."

"So, what are you saying?" asked Larry.

"I'm saying, you are fun and everybody likes you. They know you're on your way to Europe and will be gone in a few days; but, in the meantime, they hope they'll be able to see a lot of you. What are we talking about, anyway? You must have about eight invitations to lunches and dinners, as far as I can count."

Larry nodded.

George turned to Sophie. "Sophie, my dear, do you really intend to settle here in the East?"

"You bet your snakeskin boots I do."

George smiled. He liked everything about this girl. In fact, he liked her more when she let down her guard, as she was finally doing now. He realized, however, that she would have to polish her ways if she wanted to fit in with the rest of society here. "Sophie, if you want to stay in New York, you should learn some of our ways."

"I'm not sure I like your 'ways' as you call them. Like this puny little townhouse you have here. My suite at the Waldorf puts it to shame."

"Sophie!" said her sister-in-law, Julie.

"Well, it does."

"I'm a single man," George smiled as he said it. "This is very comfortable for me." He ran through the inventory. "An entrance hall, a large living room, a separate dinning room, a large kitchen, two bedrooms, a study, servants' quarters. What else do I need?"

"You forgot to mention, George, that this is also a very 'posh' neighborhood," added Julie.

George shrugged. He took that for granted.

"What are you really saying, George?" asked Sophie.

"Visiting New York for a week is fine. Everybody loves you. You're refreshing and fun, and you're obviously enjoying yourself. But if you intend to settle here, we're going to have to get a little bit of Texas out of you before you'll feel really at home."

"How?"

George scratched his forehead. "There are two ways. One is for you to go to what they call a 'finishing school,' but I don't think that's the best solution. On the other hand, I have an aunt in Boston who, I'm sure, would love to come down and teach you a few things that'll make your life here more enjoyable."

"That's a very kind offer, George. I should be insulted, but I'm not. There's another way. Why don't you be my teacher?" asked Sophie daringly. "I'd much rather learn from you."

≈

A week later, the Kingmans sailed for Europe, leaving Sophie ensconced at the Waldorf Astoria in her suite, which George had to admit was huge and luxurious. He was in a perfect position, as far as he was concerned. He was the only man Sophie knew in New York, and he'd been taking her to lunch and dinner almost every day, subtly introducing her to the civilities and the "civilized" of New York City. They never ran out of conversation. And they never stopped flirting, either.

All the while, George was negotiating with his Aunt Caroline in Boston to come down and teach Sophie to be a "lady."

"She sounds awfully raw to me," shouted Aunt Caroline into the black box of the telephone, a newly acquired contraption she used reluctantly and considered a "newfangled monster that would destroy the art of letter writing."

"I don't know if I'm up to the job."

"Unless you want to have a *gauche* niece-in-law, you had better try. I'm doing my best, but I certainly lack your feminine touch."

"It's like that, is it?"

"Yes, Aunt Caroline. I'm crazy about her, but I wish her brother hadn't told me just how rich she is. How can a comparatively poor man like me ask a rich girl like her to marry me? I just can't do it. It isn't in my nature."

"Because," snapped Caroline. "you have the bloodline and the culture. It's a perfect match. Remember what your grandfather told you: You have to make or marry money every third generation, and it's about time you did just that!"

"You surprise me, sometimes, my dear aunt. The Kingmans are one of the finest families in Texas. They went with Stephen Austin, fought beside Sam Houston at San Jacinto, rode against Comanches—"

"All right, George, all right. Enough Wild West talk. You've piqued my curiosity. But will I be staying with you at your house?"

George was silent.

"Are you there, George?"

"You could, Aunt Caroline. Sophie doesn't like my townhouse, perhaps you wouldn't either."

"What was she doing in your house, George?"

"She and her family came to a dinner party I gave for them. Gosh! You have a suspicious mind, Auntie dear."

That evening at dinner George told Sophie, "My Aunt Caroline has agreed to come. We thought it best if she stayed with you."

"Thank you, George. I'm not thrilled, but I guess it will be all right."

"Sorry you're not thrilled, Sophie, but you know the reason you should do this?"

"Yes, George. Otherwise you won't marry me."

George Phillips almost fell out of his chair. Sophie kept on eating slowly, as if she hadn't just thrown a bomb into the middle of the table.

George sputtered incoherently. But he recovered quickly. "Then you know I love you?"

"Well, of course, George Phillips. And you must know I simply adore you. I have ever since we first met."

George reached out and took her hand. For the first time in a long time, he was filled with great joy.

"Why is it that men can't say these things? You're the one who should have told me you love me, George dear, not the other way around. I certainly don't understand men. Besides me, everybody else knows you love me, too. They've asked me when we're going to get married."

George gazed into her beautiful eyes, then furrowed his brow. "Problem," he said.

"What problem? You're married already? Engaged? In love with somebody else? I couldn't stand that, you know!"

"No, no, no, darling. I love only you. The problem is that you are a very rich young lady, and I am a man with a small income and no real prospects. Just a lot of pride. And I know you'd never agree to live on my income, nor would I let you support me. Now, do you understand?"

"Yes, darling, and I wouldn't have it any other way."

George was truly perplexed by the answer but decided to let it go. Women to him were a strange breed at best.

After dinner he walked Sophie back to the Waldorf, arm in arm. "I'm glad we cleared things up," said George. "I've been wanting to tell you I adored you ever since we met. I just didn't have the courage, I suppose. But I do, Sophie. I love you more than life!"

She gave him a hug. "The nice thing is that Larry and Julie like you, too. They're extremely pleased you're going to marry me."

"How do they know?"

"I told you, *everybody* knows."

George laughed out loud. "You mean I'm the last one to know?"

Sophie smiled coquettishly, nodding her head.

At the Waldorf, George escorted Sophie up to her suite, as usual. Only this time, he did not say good night to her. After he had taken her key and opened the door for her, she took his hand and they entered her suite together. As soon as the door closed, Sophie turned her face up to George's. Very gently, he kissed her. She pulled him to her and kissed him hard. Before he knew it, his arms were around her. George was breathing very hard. His hand groped unsuccessfully for her breast. She unbuttoned the top of her starched white dress to assist him.

Breathless, Sophie gasped, "George, you're a man, and I have been married before."

Before she could suggest to George that they go to her bedroom, they were on the deep pile rug on the sitting room floor, writhing out of their clothes and into each other's arms.

It was heaven for them both. They resumed their activity in the next room an hour later, rolling naked in the large bed. George continued to kiss Sophie as they rested. They made love again and again.

It was the first night George Phillips had ever slept at the Waldorf Astoria, and he was glad Aunt Caroline wasn't there.

Late the next morning, George stretched luxuriously in bed. At that moment Sophie turned her naked body toward his. Their kisses turned to passion, their passion turned to making perfect love.

Afterward, Sophie smiled. "Now, you're mine, George," she said simply.

Although a month had passed since George's conversation with his Aunt Caroline, the older woman hadn't yet managed to settle her affairs in Boston. George and Sophie were left alone in New York to make ardent love every night and continue their "protocol and etiquette training" by day. Once, when George came to pick her up for dinner, he found her with the lights turned low and completely naked when she opened the door to let him in. He was grateful again that Aunt Caroline was not there.

After their passion was exhausted, George asked as casually as he could, "Sophie, do you really love me?"

"What do you think, George Phillips? That I sleep with every man who comes along. That certainly would not be proper etiquette! Of course, I love you, you dummy."

"Well, darling, since I've already bought the ring, suppose we get married now?"

"George, sweetheart, you're so romantic I could hit you in the mouth with a skillet. Why don't you *ask* me to marry you?"

"Sophie, I love you with all my heart and I'm asking you to do me the great honor of becoming my wife."

"Now you're talking, George. But don't say things like that unless you mean them."

"I mean every word."

Sophie leaned over and kissed him. She giggled. "I guess we can get married tomorrow, if you can wait that long."

"Hold it, darling," said George. "I have to tell my family, get my things together, tell my uncle—"

"That'll take too long, my love. We'll get married and *then* you can tell them."

"Gee," said George. "I was hoping to be able to persuade my uncle to come to our wedding."

"The President?"

"Yes," said George. "That's the one."

So it was that George Phillips was on the next train to Washington.

Roosevelt greeted his nephew warmly, and George got right to the point. "Guess what, Uncle Ted," he said, "I'm getting married."

"Congratulations, my boy! My, but you move fast. Who is she?"

"The sweetest thing you ever saw. You remember Larry Kingman, my buddy in the Rough Riders? The one I brought by to see you just before I left?"

Roosevelt nodded. "He was, and still is, the best of the best."

"Well, Larry's got a sister I'm crazy about. Sophie. You met her at the same time you met Larry and his wife. I'm going to marry her, and I want you and Aunt Edith to come to the wedding."

The president paced back and forth for a few minutes. He said, "I remember that girl—a fine specimen of womanhood. George, I think that's bully! I could tell then that you had your eye on her. But I had a mission for you. Can you fit it in before the wedding?"

"What is it, Uncle Ted?"

"Panama. We'll be getting started at the end of the year. We hired a man named John Stevens to take over and supervise the building of the canal. He's a real engineering and railroad genius. Head of a railroad out west. I'd like somebody I trust to go see how he's actually doing. You are my nephew. We charged up San Juan Hill together. I trust you."

"I heard you were going to Panama, Uncle Ted."

"You heard right. I am going. Eventually. But I want you to go before I do. Deal?"

"I'll go to Panama, if you'll come to my wedding."

"Agreed." Roosevelt smiled.

Without telling anybody but a few of George's friends who were to act as witnesses, he and Sophie were married at City Hall before George departed. They planned to have an official church wedding on his return. They agreed Sophie would buy a house and that George's aunt would move in there in lieu of George's bachelor townhouse. Little did he know that his oil-rich new bride had already purchased one of the Astor mansions on Fifth Avenue.

≈

"You're my husband now, George, darling, so you have to take me with you to Panama. Or else I won't let you go."

George was gentle but firm. "I have to go to Panama. I don't want to go, but I must. The reason I can't take you is that there's a lot of yellow fever and malaria down there, and I seem to have an immunity to it, since I've never gotten it. But you could be susceptible. You could die, you know."

"I'm sorry I said that, darling. Of course you have to go alone. I understand, and I promise I won't complain again."

Now it was George's turn to be conciliatory to his bride. "I know," he said. "Sometimes, without thinking, things just pop out."

"George, darling, you're so understanding."

"But, speaking of popping out, I believe the top of your dress is slightly unbuttoned." Thereupon, he proceeded to undo the remaining buttons. The young couple spent a perfectly lovely night together, and the next morning Sophie, with an accommodating smile on her face, agreed to be pleasant to his Aunt Caroline and finish her "training" while he was gone.

G eorge arrived in Panama in late 1905. The steam shovel work had begun in November 1904. But Stevens's predecessor, John Wallace, hadn't the slightest idea of what to do. He was a neat, bespectacled man with a well-trimmed moustache and an intelligent mind, but he didn't know where to start. Nobody had told him.

"Is this going to be a lock-and-lake canal, or a sea-level canal?" Wallace had asked George before he left to take over at Panama.

George said, "I honestly don't know."

"And you're the nephew and aide to the president. Who in hell does know? And if nobody knows what they want me to do there, what am I supposed to do? Figure it out by myself?"

George had been worried. Now in Panama, he mixed with and talked to the foremen, the laborers, the office clerks, and the sanitation men. None of them had known what to do either, but with the arrival of Stevens as the new chief engineer, things were beginning to swing into gear as smoothly as a diesel train. John Stevens, was a railroad genius of the first magnitude. He had come up the hard way as a track hand, and had quickly become railroad-builder in Mexico, Minnesota, and British Columbia.

He had survived freezing prairie winters and traveled hundreds of miles into the Rockies on snowshoes. James J. Hill had hired him in 1889 for the Great Northern Railroad. Stevens found several little-known mountain passes which saved hundreds of miles of back-breaking work and, at the same time, gave the Great Northern the lowest gradings of any railroad to the Pacific. He had built bridges, tunnels, and over a thousand miles of railroad—more than had been built by any man in the world. It was James J. Hill who recommended Stevens to Roosevelt. "He's finished his job. He's restless and wants to move on," Hill had told the president. "I've offered him the highest positions we have, but he's turned me down. He wants a challenge, not a position."

George made friends with the most intelligent man of the many he met, who happened to be a Negro labor boss. His name was Fred. "Fred what?" asked George.

"Just Fred," replied the man. They talked a lot. Fred told George how he had come to Panama from Barbados to work for the railroad. Fred was cheerfully clever. He could discuss things with George that the engineers and the planners and other workmen couldn't, or wouldn't.

"Why don't you have a last name?" George asked him.

"Why should I? Your last name is Phillips. So, people call you Mr. Phillips, don't they?"

"Well, yes, I suppose so."

"If my name was Fred Phillips, what would they call me? *Mr.* Phillips? Hell no. They'd call me Phillips. 'Hey,' they'd say, 'come here, Phillips.' See what I mean? So, I'd just as soon be called Fred. At least that's a first name. Your friends call you George, now, don't they? Well, everybody calls me Fred."

"So please call me George."

Fred started to shake his head.

"And I'll call you Mr. Fred."

They laughed. Fred said, "All right, George, as long as nobody else is around to hear me do it."

Walking along the railroad tracks on their way back from the work site, George said, "Tell me, Mr. Fred, we both believe in God, but is he a benevolent god or a malevolent god? Is he good, or is he bad?"

"Good, of course," said Fred.

"What makes you think that, Fred?" asked George. "Look at all the bad things that happen in his world. Look at Panama. Yellow fever, malaria. Consider the agony they cause. Look at the thousands who have died and will die."

The discussion went on for quite awhile. Finally, George said, "You know, Fred, there is no answer. We won't know for sure until we are dead and buried."

"Yes," said Fred. "There is an answer. God is in each one of us. We are part of him, and he is part of us. We're bad sometimes and good sometimes. We are God and God is us."

They were still walking along the railroad tracks. George stopped suddenly, as he often did when he wanted to make a point of something he was saying. He was about to raise a finger to make a comment on Fred's theory, when a shot shattered the evening stillness. Fred fell to the ground. As George stooped to cradle Fred's head and feel for his pulse, another shot whistled overhead. Seeing that Fred was dead, George ran in the direction of the shots. Several men had joined him. Nobody could have missed hearing the shots. They found nothing. No clues, nothing.

After giving his testimony at the Canal Zone Police Station, George realized that he had become very fond of Fred during their brief acquaintance. He had genuinely liked and admired the man, and he had hoped Fred would be company for him in this strange place. Once alone, George wept for his comrade.

More frightening thoughts crept in during the middle of the night. Was the gunman shooting at him or at Fred? If at Fred, was he some kind of bigot? What could Fred have done to provoke murder? The Americans had brought segregation with them to Panama, something unheard of before their arrival. Could it have been his friendship with Fred that had gotten someone so upset he'd shot him? Or could he have been trying to shoot George? And if so, why? The very notion of such a thing made George break out in a sweat.

≈

As the days progressed, George found himself becoming more than slightly neurotic. He was suspicious of everybody, on his guard all the time. He questioned innocent remarks. He opened closet doors before sitting down in a room. At a dinner, after George sharply asked an official why he intended to issue arms to the guards on the railroad, one guest commented, "George, you are getting to be obnoxious. I don't think there's anybody on the Isthmus of Panama who wouldn't gladly kill you right now."

He apologized, trying to make light of the situation by joking about how he'd have to leave before he would be involuntarily committed to an asylum. Outside, after saying good night to his host and hostess, George turned to join some friends. As he did, he tripped on an unseen porch mat. As he fell forward, a knife swished over his head and imbedded itself into the side of the house, which was made of wood like all the Canal Zone houses.

"Go," shouted George to the group. "Run! Somebody get him!"

But there was no one there. Nobody could find anything. George cursed them all. Then he realized how lucky he had been. Who in the hell would want to kill me? he wondered.

Invited to a party at the Stevens's home, George chatted innocently with a most attractive young lady. He missed Sophie dreadfully and was glad for some feminine companionship. It somehow made him feel closer to his new bride at home. The young lady was southern and her drawl fascinated him. After the party, he remained outside with her in the moonlight. He was telling her a joke, when he heard a scuffle behind them. George jumped. The woman gasped. A man in civilian clothes walked up and tipped his hat. "We got him, sir," he said.

"How did you ever come to be here?" George asked him.

"After what happened the other night, Mr. Stevens told us to keep an eye on you night and day, sir."

"And, by golly, we got our man," said another man stepping out of the shadows.

"Who is it?" asked George.

"My men have taken him down to the stationhouse, sir. We don't want to cause a commotion or anything like that."

"Yes, yes," said George. "If somebody would be kind enough to escort this young lady home, I'll be right down."

President Theodore Roosevelt, 26th U.S. president
(1901–1909), authorized the building of the Panama
Canal in 1902, considering it one of the two most
important events in U.S. history along with the
Louisiana Purchase. *(Keystone-Mast Collection,
University of California-Riverside Museum of Photography)*

Colonel George Washington Goethals, U.S. Army Corps of Engineers, Chairman and Chief Engineer, Isthmian Canal Commission, 1907–1914, Governor of the Canal Zone, 1914–1916 *(Keystone-Mast Collection, University of California-Riverside Museum of Photography)*

Colonel William Crawford Gorgas, Chief Health Officer, Isthmian Canal Commission, 1904–1910 *(Keystone-Mast Collection, University of California-Riverside Museum of Photography)*

Construction of the upper and lower locks at
Miraflores *(Keystone-Mast Collection, University of
California-Riverside Museum of Photography)*

Ships transitting the Panama Canal
(Photo by Kevin Jenkins for the Boyd
Steamship Corporation)

USS *Ohio,* moving through the Culebra Cut
on a training cruise for the U.S. Naval
Academy, October 1915 *(Keystone-Mast
Collection, University of California-Riverside
Museum of Photography)*

President Roosevelt seated in the operator's
seat of a steam shovel during his visit to
view construction progress of the Panama
Canal, November 1906 *(Keystone-Mast
Collection, University of California-Riverside
Museum of Photography)*

Panama's Revolutionary Junta on
November 4, 1903, after the formal
reading of the new country's Declaration
of Independence in the Cathedral Plaza,
Panama City. Left to right, front row:
unidentified, Federico Boyd, unidentified,
José Agustin Arango, Tomás Arias. Back
row: unidentified, James R. Shaler
*(Keystone-Mast Collection, University of
California-Riverside Museum of Photography)*

At the station, the police explained that they knew they had to catch the man quickly before he could escape the Zone into Panama, where they had no jurisdiction. Mr. Stevens had insisted that all canal operations offices, personnel quarters, and equipment be relocated from Panama City into the confines of the Canal Zone, which, of course, further divided the Panamanians from the Americans. George couldn't help but feel the country was being physically divided right down the middle.

The prisoner was light-skinned with stringy, black hair. His face was flat, like an Indian's. His eyelids half covered the wild eyes beneath them.

"Hell," said George. "He's not a Panamanian or a West Indian. I'd say he's from Central America somewhere."

"Says he doesn't speak English," said the inspector.

George attempted to restrain himself, speaking softly to the prisoner to put him at ease. He imagined, and hoped, that the police had probably been grilling him already. Although George's Spanish was not perfect, he could be understood. "Why do you want to kill me?" he asked. "I've done nothing to you. I don't even know you."

"I don't speak English," said the man in Spanish.

"I was speaking Spanish."

The man laughed. "Funny Spanish," he said.

George looked around. All the faces were American. "You must have a Spanish translator," he said to the chief inspector.

"Yes, sir. He'll be in first thing in the morning."

"Anybody here who's bilingual?" pleaded George.

"What?"

"Anybody here who speaks Spanish and English?"

"I'll get José."

While waiting, George surveyed the cracks in the floor tiles while his mind raced. He was desperate to find out why this man wanted to murder him. Could he be a relative of Chomorro who was still angry about Manuel? No. He didn't look at all like a Chomorro. Perhaps he is a Nicaraguan who is angry because he thinks I was instrumental in locating the canal in Panama instead of Nicaragua? But if that were true, he'd have gone after Bunau-Varilla, wouldn't he? But Bunau-Varilla is in Paris, and I'm in Panama. Much easier. No, this fellow is no idealist. He is just a Central American Indian who was getting paid to kill me. But why? Why?

He turned to the prisoner again. *"Porqué? Porqué quiso matarme?* Why? Why did you want to kill me?" he asked

"I don't speak English," he repeated in rapid Spanish.

George felt like killing him. "Why?" he asked again.

"Tu sabes," said the man. *"Tu sabes."*

You know. You know. But the man was using the familiar tense, which was a sign of disrespect when directed to a stranger. The prisoner was openly defying George Phillips.

All was quiet. Exasperated, George rested his head in his hands. When he finally looked up again, he remembered that the interpreter would not be arriving until morning. The equally exhausted prisoner was already asleep.

George had no idea why he should be the target of an assassin. Leaving the station, he walked slowly now that he knew the source of his fear was locked up. Lost in thought, he found himself in the vicinity of his friend Juan de la Guardia's house. It was late, but there was a light flickering in Juan's window. Juan didn't like the gas jets. Once he forgot to turn them off after dousing the flame and almost died of gas inhalation. So he still used kerosene. George had told him about Mr. Edison's invention, but Juan didn't believe it. George knocked tentatively. Juan came to the door. Surprised, he said, "Come in, my friend. Come in."

Almost before he had crossed the threshold, George came right to the point. "Why would a man, a Nicaraguan, want to murder me?"

"They caught him, then?" exclaimed Juan. Like everybody else in Panama City, he had heard about the attempts on George's life.

George nodded. "It must be the same man. He tried again tonight, and they grabbed him. But he won't offer any information. Pretends he doesn't understand English or *my* Spanish."

"Well, George, your Spanish could use a little polishing up. As to why he'd try to kill you, I don't know. Do you want me to come to the police station with you and try to get it out of him?"

"No, Juan, my friend, it's too late. I just wanted you to know."

CHAPTER

George arrived at the stationhouse early the next morning after a
restless night. The translator, José, came in a few minutes later. The
prisoner glared at them as George, José, and the chief of the Canal Zone
Police squeezed into the narrow corridor just outside his cell. "Please ask
him why he tried to kill me," said George.

After both Hispanic men spoke very rapidly, José turned and said,
"He says you know."

"That's what he said last night. I wouldn't be asking the question if
I knew the answer." George was getting irritated.

José turned and the two Latins spoke again.

"He says to tell you he is Nicaraguan."

"I can see he's Nicaraguan. Why does that make him to want to kill
me?"

More translating.

"He says that if you do not know, that is too bad. You are, excuse
me, señor, he says you are a fool."

"Ask him if he was the one who killed my Negro friend the other
day. Tell him he will hang for killing him."

"He says the gringos do not hang people who kill Negroes."

"You tell him he is very mistaken. Tell him justice works swiftly here in the Canal Zone. Tell him he will hang within the month."

After the usual machine-gun-fast chatter, the Nicaraguan still shook his head.

George turned to the chief of police, who was in uniform. "Would you please nod your head and tell him José and I are speaking the truth, sir?"

The chief complied.

The Nicaraguan shrugged.

"Please come with me," said George, motioning to the chief of police to follow him.

Outside, George said, "I have an idea. Rabies does not exist here in Panama, correct?"

Shaking his head vigorously, the chief said, "Absolutely not. We're as isolated as an island. Mountains to the west and dense jungle to the east. Impenetrable."

"Well, there is a fair amount of it in Nicaragua. I've heard of an American crossing Nicaragua on the way to California who was having a bite to eat at an outdoor cafe and reached down to pet a stray dog. The dog licked his hand, which, incidentally, had a slight cut on it. Turned out the dog was rabid. I hear the man was in such agony he screamed for five days before he finally died."

The policeman wondered how the sad tale could relate to the matter at hand.

"I'm sure you have a stationhouse dog around here," continued George. "This is a transplanted U.S. police station, and every one I've ever heard of has one."

"Sure," said the chief. "Real nice dog, too. No rabies though, thank God."

"Thank God is right," agreed George. "But, tell me, do you have any shaving soap around here?"

≈

A few minutes later, after briefing the chief about his plan, George reappeared with a plump white mongrel on a leash who was shaking his head trying to get the froth out of its mouth. "Rabid dog," said the chief, winking at José. "We've got no place to put him, so we thought we'd leave him in here with the prisoner. He won't be able to bite anybody that way. Except, of course, the criminal here."

"No!" shouted the Nicaraguan.

"Sorry, but we have to put him someplace secure," said the chief. So saying, he opened the door and pushed the dog into the cell, closing the door quickly.

The prisoner had jumped onto the cell's bunk. "No!" he screamed.

The dog continued to shake his head, spewing foam in all directions.

"Por favor!" screamed the prisoner. "Please! I promise to tell you everything. Everything! Just take this dog away."

The chief pulled the dog out of the cell and whispered to one of his men to rinse out the dog's mouth. He turned to the Nicaraguan. "All right, tell us the reason you were trying to murder Mr. Phillips here."

The man took a deep breath. He never took his eyes off George as he replied in almost perfect English. "I do it for my *patrona*, the señorita Maria. She loves an *hombre* named Manuel Chomorro. Her family, the

Lacayos, are very powerful. They do not like Manuel. But she and Manuel plan to run away together. Then this man shoot Manuel—"

"It was a fair fight," cut in George. "The courts acquitted me. I fired in self-defense."

"Who cares?" said the prisoner. "Manuel die. Maria very sad. She has temper. Get very angry. I work all my life for Lacayo family, but I like best Maria. She know that. She tell me about Mr. George Phillips. She tell me this Phillips is in Panama. She tell me, go kill Phillips. I try. God knows I try. But Phillips is like devil, hard to kill."

George's head was reeling. Maria? Good God. He sucked in his breath. He asked very softly, "Are you lying?"

The man shook his head. "No. Maria tell me you kill her lover, so I must kill you."

George nodded. He realized that, as Marion Wendell had been in the Wild West, he, too, was out of his element in this volatile country.

After the ocean trip and the overland journey, George was tired as he rode up to the Lacayo *rancho*. Dismounting, he ignored the *vaqueros* lounging around waiting for dinner. He knocked, was admitted by a *major domo* and asked to see Señor Lacayo. His old friend came to the door. Obviously surprised, Lacayo embraced George in a big *abrazo*. "My friend, *Jorge!*" he exclaimed. "I thought the next time I would see you would be in New York. I am pleased, very pleased to see you. I hope you will stay a long time."

"I'm afraid I've come with an unpleasant story," said George.

"Oh? What is it?"

"One of your employees was just sentenced to hang in Panama."

"How terrible," said Lacayo. "What crime did he commit?"

"He came to Panama for the sole purpose of murdering me. Tried several times. Succeeded in killing a friend of mine."

Out of the corner of his eye, George saw Maria descending the stairs. When she saw him, her eyes widened wildly and she put her hand to her breast. She twirled around and started back up the stairs.

"No, Maria," said George in a firm voice. "I want you to be present. I am telling your father about what happened in Panama."

But Maria had fainted.

≈

Before George Phillips returned to Panama, Señor Lacayo assured him he had arranged for Maria to marry an old but very rich man who had always wanted her as his wife and could keep her under control. The man's name was Arturo Zamora, and he was very strict. It was rumored that his last wife died after a severe beating he had given her for rearranging the furniture without his permission. George felt sorry for Maria, but she needed restraining.

CHAPTER

George stopped briefly in Panama before returning to New York. The president, he learned, was involved in discussions with his engineers as to whether they should build a sea-level canal or a lock canal. George had no opinion. As far as he was concerned, he was going to start a new life with the woman he adored. He worried about her, even though he and Sophie kept in touch by correspondence, writing each other almost every day.

On his return, there was a joyful reunion on the dock. "Let's get married," were Sophie's first words. "We don't need your uncle. If we wait for him, we'll wait a hundred years."

"I thought we *were* married," said George.

Sophie smiled. "I have good news, George. They found more oil on our property."

≈

In bed that night, after some ardent love-making, George expressed his amazement at the size of their lavish, new house. Sophie said, "Most of the oil was on my land, darling."

"So? Even though we're Mr. and Mrs. George Roosevelt Phillips, what's yours is yours."

"Are you sure you don't want to change your mind, sweetheart? My having so much money used to scare you to death."

"To hell with money. I'll take you any way you come," laughed George.

"I'm so happy you feel that way, George." Sophia looked genuinely relieved.

"Look, angel, what's the big problem?"

"There is none," said Sophie, "and that's what's so grand. You don't even care that we're now filthy rich. You don't even care."

George kissed her hard. "Darling, it's really not important. Let me just repeat that what's mine is yours and what's yours is your own. All right?"

The passion generated by George's remark was indescribably delicious.

$$\approx$$

The formal church wedding in Kingman, Texas, was a great success, elegant yet lavish, the bride resplendent in satin, the groom a statuesque figure in top hat and tails. Although President and Mrs. Roosevelt had not been able to attend, they cabled their best wishes. At the reception following the ceremony, George made a point of seeking out his friend and now brother-in-law Larry. "I'm a very lucky man," said George. "I understand Sophie's not only ravishingly beautiful, but that she's rich as hell."

Larry smiled. "They found oil on my spread, too, only I won't let them drill anymore."

George looked at his friend carefully. Larry was astute. If he didn't want the millions in oil money, there had to be a good reason. "Why not, Larry?"

Larry put his hand on his friend's shoulder. "George, my friend, every family I know in Texas who got rich quick on oil money went straight to hell. You have no idea. They become alcoholics and commit suicide. They divorce and murder each other. They make fools of themselves. You name it. So I decided I'd never let that happen to my family. Never."

"How does Julie feel?" George asked. "Wait," he interrupted. "I think I know the answer. She's going along with it."

"We talked it over and decided jointly. She's with me one hundred percent. If we ever run short and need money, we can drill as much or as little as we need to keep things going. But right now, the cattle business is good. And you know, George, the oil will keep forever right where it is. But the cattle won't."

George laughed. "You've given me food for thought, Larry. How do you think Sophie feels about it? She took the money and ran. What will she do with such a big fortune?"

"I'm not worried about Sophie. She's got *you*. She was waiting for you to come back and tell her how to invest it."

"Gosh," said George. "I married a jewel. But it's her money now. I told her she could keep it all. And I don't know what to tell her to do with it."

"You know, George, all her life Sophie's wanted to move away from Texas. Now, she's going to. Plus, she's got an ace of a husband. The money issue will work itself out. Stop worrying, brother-in-law!"

The George Phillipses began their honeymoon in New Orleans and had a splendid time strolling down the Rue Royale, shopping for antiques. George turned to his bride and said casually, "I never thought the moment would come when I felt completely satisfied."

Sophie cocked her head, "How do you mean that?"

"The way I said it. I could never look at another woman now, and I can never get enough of you. The poet Burns said it better: 'Just to know her is to love her. Love but her and love forever.' How do you like that?"

"I love it." She leaned her head against his shoulders and sighed contentedly.

The honeymooners stopped in Washington on their way home to New York. Sophie, naturally, wanted to visit the President of the United States again. Roosevelt went a step further and gave a dinner in her honor, where she mingled freely with cabinet ministers, ambassadors, and senators—in short, the cream of the cream of Washington society. And she captivated them all. She had gracefully tempered her Texas spirit with a new sophistication.

The next day, at his uncle's invitation, George Phillips went to the White House. After their greetings, George asked, "Well, Uncle Ted, are you going to build a lock-type canal or a sea-level canal? That seems to be the big issue here in Washington these days."

"I don't know. We're forming a review board to evaluate both plans. How would you like to serve on it?"

"I'm not an engineer," said George. "I'd be no help at all. Besides, I'll bet you've got it all figured out already."

Roosevelt laughed heartily. He nodded. "A lock canal will save a lot of time, George. It'll save a lot of digging. So, I say let's construct our lock canal, then we can always go back and build us a sea-level one, which will be more practical in the long run."

"So you want a canal now, the faster the better."

Roosevelt nodded.

"Then why the damned review board?"

"To be absolutely sure it can be done without error or mishap."

"You mean to take the blame if it doesn't work?"

Roosevelt said, "You'll be available to go back to Panama, won't you, nephew?"

George Phillips smiled. "I hadn't even thought of it," he said. "The last time I went, somebody tried to murder me. Now I'm a married man. I have responsibilities. I was thinking more of settling in New York again. Sophie's bought a grand new house."

"Go ahead. Go finish your honeymoon." The president grinned. "You'll be doing everybody in Washington a favor, you know. Don't think we don't all notice that you and Sophie are dying to be alone together even before they serve the first course."

"Nonsense. We behave with the utmost decorum at all times, and—"

"Some things show, whether you try to hide them or not." The president laughed again. "I might need you later, though, George. Panama's a tricky piece of work. It's going to be a tough job. So please keep in touch."

≈

George and Sophie were still unpacking in New York when Sophie asked, "Will you take me to Panama some day?"

"Darling, I'll take you tomorrow if you like. And we can both die of yellow fever together. Great way to go. First you shiver, then you turn yellow and perhaps start vomiting black—" He stopped when he saw her grimacing. "Or perhaps you prefer malaria."

She recovered her composure. "You didn't die of either, George."

"I wasn't there long enough."

"Do you know Dr. Gorgas?" Sophie's question was unexpected.

"How and where did you ever hear of Dr. Gorgas?"

"You think you married an idiot, don't you, George, dear. Well, I hate to disappoint you, but I can read and write and do all sorts of clever things like that."

"But how do you know who Dr. Gorgas is?"

Sophie playfully threw a pillow at George. "Like I said, I can read. It seems that Dr. William Crawford Gorgas and Walter Reed cleaned up Cuba and got rid of all the yellow fever and malaria there, and now Dr. Gorgas is in Panama trying to do the same thing. But he's not getting the cooperation he needs, so he can't do much; and until he does, they can't build the darned canal." Out of breath, Sophie threw herself onto a soft chair.

"Wow!" exclaimed George. "You said a mouthful! Anyway, to answer your question, I have met him. He's a very fine man and, I understand, an outstanding physician."

"And do you know what I want to do, George? I want to use our money to buy everything Dr. Gorgas needs and send it to him."

"Let's wait and see what Stevens does," suggested George. "The canal is a government project, and I don't think we can just go sending down shiploads of medical supplies without going through a lot of red tape, authorizations, permits, and all the rest."

"Suppose Stevens *doesn't* do anything?"

"Darling, be patient. I have an idea Stevens will do a lot."

On August 1, 1905, only a week after his arrival in Panama, John Stevens ordered a halt to all work in the Culebra Cut. He gave top priority to the eradication of yellow fever, malaria, and pneumonia, which were killing his men almost as fast as they arrived and crippling the progress of the canal.

Stevens approved whatever money and supplies were needed to clean up both Panama City and Colon. Under the direction of Dr. Gorgas, history's most expensive, ambitious, and successful eradication of disease began.

Gorgas, at fifty, was a gentle man with white hair and soft eyes. He wore old, wrinkled suits and might have seemed, on first glance, a harmless, ineffective sort. In truth, he commanded tremendous respect and the admiration of virtually everyone with whom he worked. It was his tactful, sensitive nature that his workers admired and to which they responded.

Stevens and Gorgas developed an immediate liking for each other, spurred in part by their shared sense of purpose. At one point, when there were recommendations being made in Washington to replace Gorgas, Stevens fought hard to keep him on. In doing so, Stevens was rewarded by Gorgas's absolute allegiance and support.

Four thousand men were recruited to work on Gorgas's project. Every crevice of Panama City and Colon was fumigated again and again. Efforts were then expanded to the rest of the country. The last death from yellow fever was reported in December. The disease had disappeared from Panama.

≈

After resuming his work on the canal, John Stevens became embroiled in Washington politics as the U.S. Senate continued vigorous debates over building a sea-level or lock canal. The fact that this critical logistical decision had not yet been resolved presented an enormous stumbling block for Stevens (and, indeed, had prompted Wallace to resign.)

A lock canal, consisting of three manmade concrete chambers, each a thousand feet long and one hundred ten feet wide, would, when filled by gravity with water flowing from an artificial lake, "lift" the vessels over the mountains, and permit them to steam across that lake to the other side of the isthmus where they would be lowered back to sea-level by another series of identical locks. A lock canal would entail much less digging but, over the years, would require far more maintenance.

Because of the mountains in central Panama, however, building a sea-level canal, according to Stevens, would require eighty-seven feet of additional excavation and ten more years of digging. And, although the end result would be significantly more efficient and require less maintenance, Stevens argued fiercely for the lock canal, feeling that a sea-level body of water at the base of two mountains would create landslides and a constant danger to ships and their passengers and crews.

At the end of 1906, Stevens traveled to Washington to argue his point. He was a rugged, handsome man with short dark hair and a bushy moustache. In his early 50s, his body was still strong and tough, still capable of enduring the most arduous conditions. His colleagues considered him immensely intelligent and, unless unfairly crossed, easy to get along with.

Stevens knew that the idea of a lock canal was not popular and flew directly in the face of a recommendation made by a panel of American and European experts. But Stevens, arguing his point with intelligence, hands-on knowledge, and unrivaled experience, made an indelible impression on the American political community. He and his colleagues won the fight. On June 21, 1906, Congress adopted the plan for a lock canal with an estimated completion date of January 1, 1915.

≈

"I knew they'd come up with plans for a lock canal," said George over breakfast. He and Sophie were now living in the grand house on Fifth Avenue in Manhattan. Coleman had come with them and was now in charge of a staff of five other servants.

"Do you approve, darling?"

"No," said George without hesitation.

"Why not?"

"Too complicated," said George.

"But, sweetheart, it seems to be a terribly hard job just to dig out the Culebra Cut. Just think how difficult it would be to dig across the whole Isthmus of Panama."

"Darling," said George, "the Cut is the hardest part of the entire project. Once that's done, the rest will be easy. Cutting a channel eighty-seven feet deeper across the rest of the Isthmus would be a piece of cake."

"You couldn't convince your uncle?"

George shook his head. "A sea-level canal would have taken longer. Been easier, but taken longer. Did you ever know Uncle Ted not to be in a hurry?"

≈

Work began in earnest once the plan was ratified by Congress. Many challenges lay ahead. For example, a solution had to be found to get rid of all the dirt and rock that was being excavated. Stevens used the experience he gained building railroads—he had laid hundreds of miles of railroad tracks through rugged mountains—to solve the problem. He expanded the Panama Railroad and scheduled trains to carry the loads quickly and expediently out of the area. Trains full of debris left every five minutes, always leaving loaded and returning empty.

At the end of October 1906, with yellow fever eradicated, George and Sophie Phillips arrived in Panama to arrange for the visit of the President and First Lady of the United States. John Stevens received the Phillipses politely but made no secret of the fact that he had more important things to do than entertain the president. Assigned one of the quarters used to house the high officials of the Canal Zone, Sophie's first words were, "George, this is simply dreadful."

"Seems fine to me," said George. "It's open and spacious."

"And all screened in," said Sophie. "And, look. It's raining."

"Of course it's raining. This is October. It's one of the rainiest months of the year."

"What are the least rainy months?"

"January, February, and March. Practically never rains then."

Sophie sat down in silence. "It rains for nine months?"

"More or less, darling."

"Good God! And your uncle's talking about leaving us here when he goes back to Washington?"

George nodded. "Just to make sure everything gets done the way he wants it."

"Don't stay *too* long, George, because I'm going to miss you a lot *after I go back with the Roosevelts.*"

George took her gently by the shoulders and looked her straight in the eye. "Sophie, darling, *you* wanted to come on this trip. It was against my better judgment, but I brought you. I figured you for a *Texan,* not a weepy little Eastern housewife. You begged to come, and now you're going to stay as long as I do. Is that clear?"

"Yes, George."

"Good."

"May I bring a few things down from New York to make this house more livable?"

"Certainly, darling. Anything that will make you happy."

≈

Theodore Roosevelt was the first U.S. president in office ever to leave the United States to visit a foreign country. The trip was the talk of the country, the subject of banner headlines. The Roosevelts sailed on November 9, 1906, on the *Louisiana* accompanied by his personal doctor, Presley Rixey of the Navy, and three Secret Service men. Two other ships, the *Tennessee* and the *Washington,* accompanied them. The sea was calm, the weather good.

The Tivoli Hotel, constructed of wood, was rushed to completion to accommodate them. Roosevelt had chosen to come during the height of the rainy season; he wanted to see Panama at its worst. He wasn't disappointed. It rained incessantly. It was raining when he arrived. And it was raining when he rode through Panama City with President Amador in an open carriage.

Stevens had organized a fairly leisurely schedule, which Roosevelt ignored, racing from place to place, wanting to see everything. Usually George accompanied his uncle, and, if there was space and the occasion warranted it, Sophie went along as a companion to Mrs. Roosevelt. On day one of his three-day visit, the president sneaked away with Gorgas to inspect the Ancon Hospital, toured the bay of Panama in a tug, ate with Mrs. Roosevelt (unannounced) at an employees' mess hall, traipsed through the Cut where railway lines were actually underwater at several points, and visited villages "knee-deep" in mud. He also witnessed a small landslide that occurred in the Culebra Cut at Paraíso. Always walking in mud, the president made speeches in the rain.

On the second day, he climbed aboard the Bucyrus steam shovel where it was preparing for the pouring of concrete for the locks at Pedro Miguel for the famous photos, which were sent out to all the newspapers of the world. It made it look as if Theodore Roosevelt was actually digging the canal. In fact, he was on the shovel for twenty minutes.

Overall, it was a magical trip from which Roosevelt returned with great enthusiasm for the project. To George he confided, "I am greatly impressed with Stevens's work. He's the man for the job, all right. He's got the exact qualifications to get this canal built."

"Yes, sir. For the short time I've been here, I have come to the same conclusion."

"But I am more fascinated by the work of Dr. Gorgas and what he's done in sanitizing the area. The death rate is now practically zero. He's made this place habitable. *He* is the one who has made this canal feasible."

"There's no doubt about that," agreed George.

"I want you to stay, George. Not forever. Not even for long. But long enough to be sure that after I've returned home, this work continues to proceed at the same pace it is going now."

"It will, Uncle Ted. But I'll stay a month or two to make sure." It turned out to be a lot longer than that.

Work in the Culebra Cut moved forward even more quickly than expected. More than half a million cubic yards of fill were being removed each month. Both in Panama and in Washington, John Stevens unanimously and deservedly received the credit for the progress. He was the right man in the right job. Some ventured to say he was the only man who could build the canal. His progress and accomplishments were phenomenal. He was the man who actually made the "dirt fly."

Then, unexpectedly, on January 30, 1907, Stevens wrote to Roosevelt conveying his deep unhappiness. He was tired, he claimed—underpaid and unenthusiastic about continuing. Although it was not a formal letter of resignation, Roosevelt regarded it as such and with some ill will, cabled back that his resignation had been accepted.

It was generally agreed among those who knew Stevens that he had become bored after solving all the problems and getting the construction well-organized and successfully underway. He'd done the hard part. The routine part of finishing the job was repetitive and dull, nothing more than digging dirt and pouring concrete. He wanted to move on to something more challenging. With Stevens, this was typical. All his life he had sought out the hard assignments, the difficult tasks. Then, after solving them, he became restless and wanted to move on, just as he had with the Great Northern and every other project he had worked on. Without him, there would not have been a canal.

George Phillips went to Stevens's office. "Sir, won't you reconsider? I know my uncle would take you back at the snap of a finger."

"You know he wouldn't," said Stevens. "He'd never back down."

"I could talk to him, sir."

"No, George. It's time for me to move on. The president knows it, and I know it."

And that was that.

Without much hesitation, Roosevelt accepted Secretary of War William Howard Taft's recommendation to appoint Colonel George Washington Goethals to take over. Goethals was forty-eight at the time, with an engineering and military background. He was tall and thin with a somewhat distant, stiff demeanor. His eyes were vivid blue, his hair silver and parted smartly down the middle. Taft had recommended him for the job once before.

George Phillips journeyed back to Washington to talk to the president, and to allow Sophie to buy some things she needed and to visit with her friends. During her trips to Washington, Sophie had made a host of friends who were all dying to hear about Panama.

George sat back contemplatively in a leather chair in Roosevelt's office. "Don't you think you should appoint a civilian?" asked George. "Why an army officer?"

Roosevelt winked. "Because an officer in the United States Army can't resign on me. I've had it with these people who come aboard for a couple of years, then quit. Goethals will be in charge until the job is finished."

≈

On March 31, 1907, George W. Goethals assumed his post as Chief Engineer and General Superintendent of the Panama Canal. Soon thereafter, Stevens departed the Isthmus of Panama by ship, leaving behind a pier jammed with people cheering him.

Goethals received a decidedly cool reception from Panamanians and canal workers alike. The public, including those working on the canal, felt a deep loyalty to Stevens and hated to see him leave. Their attitude toward Goethals bordered on hostility, coupled with a general feeling of disrespect for his career as a military engineer. Some civil engineers even walked off the job in protest, if only temporarily. To make matters worse, Goethals had none of the charisma or warmth that Stevens exuded. Yet, in the end, it was Goethals who would be hailed as the Builder of the Panama Canal. It was Goethals who would get credit as the hero of the enterprise. As one of the many subsequent tributes written in his honor proclaimed, "A man stood up in Panama/And the mountains stood aside." He would be hailed in the United States, in Panama, and throughout the world for his work, his ability and his unwavering commitment.

But such accolades were not yet forthcoming. Goethals stoically took over the job of overseeing and running the operation at the Cut, ignoring his many critics and ill-wishers. Within months, however, he won the respect, if not the devotion, of his workers. He was never well-liked but managed to instill in his men the desire to work hard and well. Among them, he became known, with guarded affection, as "The Old Man." He frequently appeared onsite, arriving in his small yellow railroad car dubbed "The Yellow Peril."

The amount of dirt that had to be removed from the Culebra Cut was unimaginable and the responsibility for the endless excavation fell solely on Goethals' shoulders. George Phillips spent most of his time sitting on a shooting stick watching the work in progress. It was astonishing to see the tremendous amount of dirt being dug by the giant Bucyrus steam shovels, three times the size of the ones used by the French. On October 4, 1907, George, perched under his umbrella that helped thwart the effects of the incessant rain, sat watching the work site opposite the Cucaracha Reach. It had been raining heavily. His shoes wore slimy overshoes of mud.

He felt rather than heard the rumble. He looked around him. Across the excavation he saw Contractor's Hill start to move. The mud and stones began to slide downhill. They gained momentum, moving slowly and ponderously, but moving inexorably toward the bottom of the Cut. George yelled at the men in the path of the slide, but they couldn't hear him. No matter. They saw what was happening and were bolting for safety. In amazement, George watched the massive landslide destroy two steam shovels and turn the railroad tracks into twisted heaps, like so much spaghetti on a plate. He felt the rumble and deafening roar of steam shovels and railroad engines colliding with each other, pushed by the dirt and debris. He looked up to see still more earth falling down the cliff, gathering both mass and speed. The workers below were running for their lives. By now, soil, mud, rock, and branches covered the machinery. George was stunned, as he watched the huge amounts of mud slowly settle to the ground, the people were straining to learn if their fellow workers were among the dead or the living. To George, it seemed almost like a battle zone. He felt small and insignificant having witnessed the awesome power of nature. And he knew it could happen again.

When the slipping stopped, 500,000 cubic yards of mud had been dumped back into the canal dig. In 1910, the same spot would suffer two more big slides. Though many thought they'd seen the worst of the slides, as the Cut grew deeper and deeper, the slides occurred more often, year after year, greatly impeding their progress.

The advisory board in its 1906 study had placed the total volume of excavation still to be accomplished at not quite 54,000,000 cubic yards. But by 1908 that estimate had to be revised to about 78,000,000 cubic yards. In 1910 it was put at 84,000,000. In 1911, at 89,000,000. By 1913 the estimate had reached 100,000,000 cubic yards, or nearly equal to the figure initially given by the advisory board for a canal at sea level!

The trouble was that after a Herculean amount of digging with the giant Bucyrus steam shovels, time after time what appeared to be the whole side of the mountain seemed to slide into the excavation, as it had during the "Cucaracha Slide," twisting railroad tracks, overturning locomotives and open freight cars, and making what amounted to a hill of mud right in the middle of the Cut. It was frustrating work. Colonel

David Gaylord, in direct charge of the cut excavation had to be sent home, where he died of a brain tumor.

≈

The Phillips's months in Panama had turned into almost a year. Sophie made the best of things. There were no children yet, although they had "practiced" regularly and cheerfully. George came home one evening, tired and dirty from his day at the Cut. He blinked. The standard superintendent's house had been transformed into a beautifully decorated home, more like Fifth Avenue than the Canal Zone. "What have you done?" he asked Sophie, who was standing in the middle of the living room.

"Remember the things I said I was going to bring down from New York? Well now this place is more livable for you," she replied sweetly.

George smiled but couldn't hide his concern. "Remember, darling, the discussion I had with Mr. Stevens? That I felt he should keep his headquarters in Panama City? Keep in touch with the local situation and the people?"

Sophie nodded.

"He told me he wanted to be where the action was. He wanted to concentrate on building the canal. Let the State Department handle Panama."

"And you said it was divisive," she reminded him. "You said that having two separate countries of sorts here in this little place was bad for morale, and the people from the States ought to mix and mingle with their hosts here in Panama."

"Well, darling, I think we better rethink our role here."

"What do you mean?"

"You see, all the people who are building the canal are working hard to do a really big job. None of them—with maybe a couple of exceptions—are rich. They all live alike, in the same type of house, with the same type of furniture. They all buy from the government commissaries and eat at the government club houses."

"It's very boring, isn't it, George?"

George had to think about that. Slowly, he said, "Yes, darling, it must be pretty dull for you. I've been an unthinking oaf. What'll we do about it?"

"George! Can't you see what I've done about it? I've made this place a decent place to live in."

"Yes, dear, but it's out of place here in the Canal Zone. 'Ostentatious' is the word they'll use to describe the Phillips's home." Sophie's face was crestfallen. "I'll tell you what we'll do. We'll move Mr. and Mrs. George R. Phillips into Panama City where we can 'mix and mingle' and do a little of our own brand of diplomacy."

Sophie threw her arms around George's neck and hugged him hard.

Only a few miles away geographically, but a world apart in perceived culture, the Phillipses found a lovely home in downtown Panama City. With the aid of a local decorator who was able to use the material and furniture Sophie had ordered from New York, they ended up with one of the loveliest residences in Panama City. With the help of Juan de la Guardia and his charming wife, Dolores, they made friends easily and soon found themselves moving more and more in Panamanian circles. "You know, George, I think the Panamanians are just grand people. I wish we had moved to Panama City when we first arrived."

As often happened, Sophie's remark caught George completely by surprise. "Well, now, Sophie darling, we came here specifically to prepare for Uncle Ted's visit; and, except for the state dinner with President Amador, the purpose of the visit was to see how the canal work was progressing. Since Uncle Ted was in the Canal Zone, *we* had to be in the Canal Zone."

"Why didn't they put us in the Tivoli Hotel with Uncle Ted?"

"I guess he wanted us to have more ample quarters than a hotel room provided. That's why he got us that big house on the hill."

Sophie made a face. "It was awful. I felt really out of place there."

"You hid it well, darling. But now we've moved into the real Panama."

"All the really nice people live here in Panama City. Those earnest people building the stupid canal are . . . are what, George?"

"Hard working, competent, American engineers, devoted to their jobs."

She ignored the sarcasm. "You know what, George? I'm glad to get away from all that 'Silver' and 'Gold' jargon, too."

George bit his lip. He knew damned well what Sophie was talking about. The United States was a strictly segregated country. White people and black people never mixed. But in Panama City, as in the rest of the country, there was no such distinction, and signs such as "Whites only" and "Negro" were considered offensive. In the Canal Zone, a more euphemistically subtle distinction took place. White workers were paid in gold and Negro workers in silver. The signs were changed to "Silver Women's Toilet," "Gold Men's Toilet," "Silver Waiting Room," and "Gold Commissary," *ad infinitum*. "It's sort of the law," said George. "Like Texas."

Sophie had to think for a minute on that one. "But we treat them differently in Texas," she said.

Slowly, Panama City was becoming a cosmopolitan center. On the upper levels of society, cultures and backgrounds were beginning to blend. Foreign businesses were coming in with foreign managers. New commercial enterprises were flourishing. Even though private enterprise was prohibited within the Canal Zone, entrepreneurs had no trouble operating from bases in Panama City and Colon. The most prominent Panamanian families, people such as the de la Guardias, mixed easily with the moneyed and well-born outsiders. They had much in common. George and Sophie were, of course, included in everything. Sophie gloried in it. George was wearing himself out, going to dinner parties and playing bridge until midnight, then getting up and going to the Canal Zone work sites. The work on the Cut was progressing faster than expected, and George knew it was time to start thinking of going back to the States.

"Sophie," he said one Sunday morning, "We're leaving. Going home."

"Oh, George! Just when I was beginning to have the time of my life!"

"Sorry, dearest, but I have orders." His statement was not entirely true, but he knew his job was over and he ought to report back to the president.

There was silence for a moment as Sophie sucked in her breath. "George," she said softly. "I'm going to have a baby."

George jumped up so fast his coffee cup fell over. "How marvelous!" he exclaimed as soon as he could talk. He leaned across the table and kissed his wife.

"We've been so happy by ourselves. I—I thought you might be angry."

"Not if the kid looks like me, I won't."

"You're about to get hit in the mouth with that skillet!"

By now, they were hugging each other. "You seem to like to hug me a lot, don't you, George."

"That's why you're pregnant, my pet."

"I didn't know that was how women got pregnant."

"You'll be on the first boat out of Panama for New York. I'll finish up here and be right behind you."

A s Chief Engineer, Goethals wanted to be responsive to his workers and to that end, he started a local newspaper, encouraging free speech and constructive criticism. He sat at an outside desk every Sunday morning and urged his men to come before him with their complaints.

They came. Most brought domestic problems. Men brought complaints against their women and women against their men. When the Old Man found out that most of the complainants were not even married, he decreed that any couple living together in canal housing had to get married immediately or move to housing outside the Canal Zone, which was much more expensive. Several hundred wedding parties began to take place every Sunday, with the brides wearing long white gowns, and the couples followed by their five or six children.

Sometimes the grievances were serious. There were knife fights, wife beatings, thefts, and other assorted crimes. They were dealt with swiftly. The more contentious were deported from the Isthmus. The Old Man's decisions were final, and there was no appeal. Most of the complaints had to do with no more than barking dogs, crying children, or lack of meat in the commissaries. These, too, were handled expeditiously.

An urgent cable from Havana reached George Phillips soon after Sophie left: COME AT ONCE. MRS. PHILLIPS BADLY INJURED IN ACCI-DENT, IN COMA. It was signed by the American consul.

George was frantic. He knew that Sophie's ship would have stopped in Havana, as most did, to pick up more cargo and passengers. But what could have happened to Sophie? George cabled the president, told him what had happened, and requested immediate leave to get to Havana as fast as he could.

His first stop in Havana was the American Legation. Havana was a much larger city than George had supposed, but he managed to hail a carriage and give instructions in his rudimentary Spanish. "Yes, sir," said the consul, shaking his hand. "We had orders from the secretary of state, himself, to get Mrs. Phillps the very best care."

"But where is she? How did this happen?" he demanded.

"Please, sir, we are doing everything for your wife that we can. She is not far from here."

"Will you take me to her?"

"Only after you allow me to explain what happened."

George stared expectantly, trying to hide his impatience. He tapped his fingers on his lap as the consul pondered how to begin.

"Mrs. Phillips left the ship with her companion, Mrs. Ewing, and hired a horse carriage to see the sights. They went to a hotel and refreshed themselves with a lemon squash."

"Yes, That would be just like Sophie. She loves lemon squash."

"Then," the consul continued, "she saw something on the other side of the street and decided to go over for a closer look. Halfway across, one of Cuba's leading citizens, Francisco Machado, came rushing down the street in his coach, his coachman driving much too fast. You can imagine the results, Mr. Phillips."

George felt his heart stop.

He must have turned chalk-white because the consul hastened to say, "She was not killed. But she was badly hurt. Señor Machado took her in his own carriage to *Las Mercedes* hospital. She remained there for a week. Señor Machado paid for everything, of course."

"Where is she now?"

"She is at the Machado home."

"Why?" George shot the question out fast.

The consul looked George in the eye. "Because, Mr. Phillips, she remembers nothing. Señor Machado feels personally responsible and has insisted that his family can look after her better than any hospital here."

"You mean she has amnesia?"

"When she fell under the horses, she hit her head."

"Will you take me to her?"

"We'll go now."

When they arrived at the Machado mansion, the door was opened by a liveried servant who announced George and the consul. A distinguished gentleman appeared almost at once. He greeted both men with great concern on his face.

"Mr. Phillips, I am so glad you have arrived. I cannot tell you how profoundly sorry I am over this grievous accident. We have done everything we can to make your wife comfortable, but we are so hopeful that seeing you will restore her memory," he said.

"Thank you, señor. I'm sure you have done your best. But please let me see her. I've been almost beside myself since the cablegram arrived. And where is Mrs. Phillips's companion, Mrs. Ewing?"

"She was on her way to visit her sick mother and had to depart. We assured her that Mrs. Phillips was in good hands and perfectly safe.

"Let us go in to see her now," Machado said. "My wife is looking after her. It was a dreadful thing, sir, a dreadful thing."

The Cuban opened the bedroom door and George rushed through. On the bed lay his Sophie.

"Darling," he whispered, with tears in his eyes. Sophie looked at him as if she had never seen him before.

George glanced back at the other two men. They were talking fast in Spanish. Seeing George's look, Machado said, "She remembers nothing. She can talk, of course. She now knows me and my wife and our three daughters and, of course, the servants."

"What's the prognosis?" asked George.

"Our doctor sees her every day. At first, she had bruises and cuts and a bump on her head. Then the doctor found she had no memory. He says it should return. He has seen this type of head injury before and says that one day, soon, of course, something will remind her of her past, and she will suddenly remember everything. All at once, it will be as it was, except, perhaps, for this period in which she has no memory."

"There are no permanent injuries, then?" George asked.

Machado was grave. "I should have told you that first. Everything seems to be fine except that she has lost the baby. But she will be all right. I believe, sir, I am more damaged than your wife. My injury is here," he said, pointing to his heart. "It was a terrible thing to happen, and I cannot but feel responsible."

"No, Señor Machado, I understand it was an accident," said George, resisting the impulse to lash out at this man for his reckless driving. He said only, "Thank you for taking care of my wife."

After the doctor visited Sophie, he assured George that she was recovering physically and that, in all likelihood, she would be able to have another baby. And he told him it would be safe for her to travel. George quickly booked passage in two staterooms on the next ship to New York and hired a nurse to care for Sophie on the journey.

As the ship sailed away from Havana, George asked the nurse to bring Sophie on deck, settle her with a book in a deck chair, and leave them alone for awhile. He sat down casually in the chair next to Sophie's, nodded pleasantly to her, and introduced himself. Sophie looked at him blankly, and said, "I'm Mary Lou Smith." She smiled at her own quick thinking.

"I believe we've met, haven't we?" asked George.

"Perhaps, but I don't really remember." With that, Sophie went back to her reading—a book he had bought in Havana written in English and titled *The War with Spain*. Because he could find nothing on the Panama Canal, he had bought the next best thing and had put it in her stateroom deliberately.

They sat in silence for some time. Sophie seemed to have nothing more to say to him, preferring to sit peacefully reading. Beginning to despair, George got up from his deck chair. "Going to take a walk around the ship," he said by way of an excuse for leaving.

Sophie nodded pleasantly.

For half an hour George stood by the rail looking at the sea. He inhaled deeply, telling himself that everything would be all right. He was almost hypnotized by the movement and the variety of the waves. The ship's bow cut the water, sending spray flying. The wake made a white line in the water, straight as an arrow. George shook his head to clear it. He was really falling under the spell of the view, but it gave him some momentary peace.

He walked slowly back to his deck chair and sat down sadly beside his beloved wife. This was going to be a long ordeal, he knew.

Suddenly, Sophie looked up and said, "George, where in the world have you been? Honestly, you can never just sit still and relax."

George looked intently at Sophie. Could it be? Was she back so suddenly? What had triggered this sudden recovery? Oh, who cared? George was ecstatic.

"I've just been for a stroll, my darling," he said happily. "You were dreaming and I didn't want to disturb you. But I'm here now, dearest, and I'll never leave you alone again."

Sophie smiled fondly at her husband and returned to her reading as calmly as if nothing had happened.

Their final adventure with the Panama Canal was over.

A few weeks later, relieved that Sophie was her former, unpredictable self once again, George traveled alone to Washington. He examined canal figures with his uncle. The cost of the canal was enormous. No single construction effort in American history had exacted such a price in dollars or in human life. Dollar expenditures since 1904 totaled $352 million (including the $10 million paid to Panama and the $40 million paid to *Compagnie Nouvelle*). Taken together, the French and American expenditures came to about $639 million. This was more than four times what Suez had cost, without even considering the sums spent by the two preceding French companies, and far beyond the cost of anything ever before built by the United States government. Except for wars, the only comparable federal expenditures up to the year 1914 had been for the acquisition of new territories, and the figure for *all* acquisitions as of that date—those for the Louisiana Purchase (which doubled the size of the then United States), Florida, California, New Mexico and other western land acquired from Mexico, the Gadsden Purchase, Alaska, and the Philippines—was $75,000,000, or only about one-fifth of what had been spent on the canal. George read the figures, then looked up at his uncle.

He shook his head, then quickly perking up, he said, "The initial cost was staggering if you look at it on a per acre basis. But remember what John Jacob Astor said when they asked him what his criteria was for making so much money in real estate? He told them there were three things to look for: Number one, location, number two, location, and number three, location."

"Bully!" exclaimed Roosevelt.

"And if we haven't procured the choicest location in the entire world, I'll eat the White House with a spoon."

The president leaned back in his chair. "The only thing is, George, we don't actually own it."

"It may be leased," ventured George "but what it really is is a grant."

≈

But the costs continued to soar. By 1907 there were thirty-two thousand people on the payroll, about eight thousand more than when Goethals took over. By 1910, after Roosevelt left the White House, there would be nearly forty thousand.

The construction of the canal would consume more than 61,000,000 pounds of dynamite. In an average month, the aggregate depth of the dynamite holes drilled in the Culebra Cut was 345,223 feet, or more than sixty-five miles, into which more than 800,000 dynamite sticks were placed by hand and more than 400,000 pounds of dynamite were exploded.

Because of the difficulty in gauging how much dynamite to use and the pace of the work, accidents were frequent and deadly. The West Indians suffered the highest number of casualties.

Not one part of the operation—not the drilling, the blasting, the shoveling, or the dirt hauling—could ever be permitted to interfere with or disrupt another.

The dumping grounds—the other end of the system—were located anywhere from one to twenty-three miles from the Cut. A very considerable part of spill served to build earth dams, embankments on the new line of the railroad, and to create the huge breakwater at the Pacific end.

≈

Although Dr. Gorgas had gotten along well with Stevens, his relationship with Goethals was another matter. The two men were not openly hostile to each other, but underlying tension was always present. Gorgas's wife, Marie, felt that Goethals' massive ego was matched only by his obsessive thirst for power, characteristics that alienated him from his colleagues, including her husband. Goethals' tall wife didn't help the couple's popularity. Effie Rodman Goethals was perceived as a haughty, vain woman who was very much in evidence, despite her distaste for life in the Canal Zone.

The two men argued over finances. Goethals was concerned about the massive expenditures in all areas, including the Sanitation Department. At one point Goethals said with exasperation, "Do you know, Gorgas, that every mosquito you kill costs the United States government ten dollars?"

Gorgas answered, "But just think, one of those ten-dollar mosquitoes might bite you, and what a loss that would be to the country."

≈

As completion of the canal drew ever nearer, and people in the United States began to realize that this long-time dream would soon become a reality, their interest and enthusiasm mounted. It was the building of the massive locks that particularly fascinated people and provided them with a real visual sense of how the canal would work.

The locks were constructed over four years, out of concrete, with thousands of moving parts. The walls of the Panama locks were poured from overhead, bucket by bucket, into gigantic forms. The fundamental element to be reckoned with and utilized in the locks, in fact the vital factor in the whole plan and all its structural, mechanical, and electrical components, was water. Water would lift and lower the ships. The buoyancy of water would make the tremendous lock gates—two to three times heavier than any ever built before—virtually weightless.

≈

The locks were completed in May 1913, nearly a year earlier than anticipated. The Culebra Cut measured eighty-seven feet above sea level.

On the afternoon of October 10, in a brilliant publicity stunt, Woodrow Wilson, who had been elected president in 1912, pressed a button in Washington and the dike that separated the two oceans at a place called Gamboa was blown sky-high. The signal, relayed by telegraph wire, was almost instantaneous. Several hundred charges of dynamite opened a hole more than a hundred feet wide. But near the center of the Cut, the Cucaracha held firm and continued to separate the two oceans. Only painstaking dredging and excavating by a force of two hundred men could break through the clay barrier. At last, on October 24, a trickle of water grew to a flow and the Cut became an extension of Gatun Lake. Panama was, as of that moment, *divided*. The continent of North America was separated from that of South America by a thin ribbon of water.

On August 15, 1914, the SS *Ancon* made the first official trip through the Panama Canal with little fanfare. Although the United States hoped for and planned a huge ceremony as the first ship formally transited the canal, it was not to be. By tragic coincidence the long effort at Panama and the long reign of peace in Europe drew to a close at precisely the same time. The headlines screamed *"WAR."* The official declaration that the Panama Canal was open to the world was buried in the back pages.

PART TWO

CHAPTER

A s the Panama Canal served the world's ships, the ill-will engendered by the Hay–Bunau-Varilla Treaty—500 square miles of Panamanian territory administered exclusively by the United States to the exclusion of any participation by Panama—festered in the hearts of all Panamanians.

George Phillips's fears about the troubles the Hay–Bunau-Varilla Treaty would cause were only too sound. Before the canal was finished, the Panamanians realized that their country had essentially been divided by a foreign power. It was as if the French or Brazilians had sovereignty for five miles on either side of the Mississippi River to the exclusion of any United States jurisdiction.

The Canal Zone operated as if it were a state of the United States. American citizens served as governors, heads of departments, foremen and artisans. The courts were American, as were the police force, the immigration and customs branches, and the postal service. Commissaries were full of U.S. products from food to cigarettes. The official language was English. It was true, George Phillips conceded, that the Canal Zone was immaculately maintained. The lawns were green and always cut to perfection, the buildings solid and freshly painted every two years, electrical and plumbing services flawless. In short, the Panama Canal Zone was a paradise. A paradise built on profit.

The Panamanians resented everything about it. It wasn't long before the unrest manifested itself in uprisings and revolts. U.S. troops were sent in to quell these "small disturbances."

≈

To their delight, Sophie gave birth to a baby boy in 1918. Before his arrival, the Phillipses were a happy and popular couple and had established a regular pattern in their lives, mostly in New York but a good six months in Texas every three years or so. But having a baby in the house was something new. The first order of business was to find suitable nurses to care for the child. They employed three who worked on eight-hour shifts. Only after the nurses were secured did George ask, "What will we name him?"

"It should be after somebody in your family or mine," said Sophie.

"Yours, then," said George. "Since Larry and Julie don't have children, how about Larry Kingman Phillips?"

"That would be grand, George, darling." Sophie paused. "But do you know what would please Larry even more? If we named him for Larry's and my father. We both worshipped him."

"What was his name, again?" asked George rather uncertainly.

"Billy Buckeroo," laughed Sophie. "Really, George. That's how he was known! Those days in the West, everybody who was anybody had a nickname. Buffalo Bill, Wild Bill Hickock, Pawnee Bill, Billy the Kid, you know. Your name is what distinguished you." George still looked uncertain.

"Relax, darling," she said. "His real name was William Kingman, and he's the one responsible for building up the ranch and all."

"William Kingman Phillips," said George, relieved. "I like it!"

Like many parents who have children late in marriage, Sophie and George couldn't get enough of young Billy. If it weren't necessary for him to have his afternoon nap, they would have spent all afternoons on the playground with him.

Their fortune continued to grow, and was even unaffected by the Wall Street crash of 1929. By 1933, George was 55, white-haired, and no longer had to work. He and Sophie spent their afternoons walking in the park and shopping. George did the walking, Sophie the shopping. Billy was in school by then.

Most evenings they went out to black-tie dinners and played bridge until two or three in the morning, hardly ever rising until noon. George was in great demand for his stories about the famous Panama Canal. He was able to make it sound as if he had been in charge of the project, and George Goethals and Dr. Gorgas and the rest were there only to assist him. He made it sound very exotic and his friends loved it, although his beloved Sophie was known to stifle a yawn now and then during the telling of a story she had heard fifty times before.

Their only child, William "Billy" Kingman Phillips, continued to grow and left for prep school at Andover in 1932 at the age of fourteen.

≈

December 7, 1941. Pearl Harbor. Another war for the Phillips family. Billy, who had graduated from Harvard in 1940, abandoned his law school education to enlist in the war. After infantry basic training and officers' candidate school, Billy went overseas as an infantry lieutenant. He tried to wangle his way into the First Infantry Division of which his cousin,

Theodore Roosevelt, Jr., was assistant division commander. Ted was a brigadier general who had earned a reputation as a combat general. After its successful campaigns in the Mediterranean, the First Division had been brought to England to train and receive equipment and replacements, including junior officers, for the invasion of the European mainland. But cousin Ted had been transferred to the Fourth Division as assistant division commander. His outstanding record was the only thing that saved him from a court martial when the army brass discovered that in Tunisia he'd told his infantry that as soon as they took Tunis they could all go back and beat up every M.P. in Oran.

But when Lieutenant Billy Phillips arrived in England, the First Division still needed junior officers badly after their losses in the North African and Sicilian campaigns, and that is where Billy was assigned.

≈

Crowded on a landing craft full of infantrymen, Billy could look over the bow and glimpse the beach whenever a wave brought the boat up or down far enough. What he saw made his stomach knot. His innate intelligence told him the enemy could hit anything that moved on that beach. They were tearing it apart from one end to the other. And there were so many dead, so many, some floating past in the water, most spread over the beach like hunks of seaweed the tide had brought in and deposited before going back for more. Billy was glad he hadn't had to go in with the first wave. He wondered if any of them were still alive. But this was bad enough. The ramp dropped into the water. Lieutenant Billy Phillips froze for a few seconds, then yelled, "Let's go! Men, let's go!" Wading the few yards into shore was like a nightmare. He wanted to dash forward as quickly as possible, but could only plod in slow-motion, weighted-down by the saltwater. Finally he felt solid ground beneath his feet. Now he could run forward, and he did, just as fast as he could, hitting the ground and rolling over to make himself a hard-to-hit-target. Still, he could hear the bullets buzzing past him like a swarm of wasps. Shrapnel from exploding shells hissed over his supine body. Some were so close, they felt like some-body snatching at his uniform. Then up and forward. He kept waving his right arm at those behind him, while shouting, "Follow me! Follow me!"

He was gaining ground. The bluffs were clearly within reach. Get-ting to his feet for a final forward dash, he felt as if someone had hit him in the leg with a sledgehammer. He went down head first, cutting his face and scalp. His steel helmet rolled a few feet away from him. He felt the blood soaking into his trousers, yet he was too stunned to do anything. He heard one of his men yelling, "Medic! Medic! Over here!" Then Billy passed out.

In the hospital in England, he learned that his cousin Ted had been awarded the two things he wanted most: the Congressional Medal of Honor and command of a division. The irony of it was that Ted Roosevelt had died of a heart attack before he could leave Normandy and never learned he had been so honored by the army in which he served so well.

꞊

After being discharged from the army in 1944 for the disabling wounds he received in Normandy, Billy decided to take the Foreign Service exam. He easily passed it, and became a State Department officer. Since the Phillips's fortune was still immense, Billy donated his entire salary to char-ities. Also, because of his wealth and background, he was stationed in

Washington. There he would be handy in case an ambassadorial post, which required large expenditures on the part of the ambassador, needed to be filled quickly. He was also considered to be of great diplomatic value because of his great uncle's and father's part in U.S. diplomatic dealings with Panama. He was often asked to supply diplomatic expertise in issues pertaining to the canal. In such cases, he always referred to his father's notes.

In 1949, at the age of 31, Billy married an intelligent, well-educated young woman named Victoria Holmes. She, like the Phillipses, was from Boston and was, in fact, distantly related to Billy. Their respective families were delighted with the match.

Victoria was the perfect mate for Billy. A willowy brunette, she was neat, fit and, while not beautiful, was most pleasing to contemplate. Her eyes sparkled with intelligence, and they were not deceiving. She was smart. They had met when Billy was at Harvard and Victoria was at Smith. Despite their mutual interest in scholarship, it didn't take them long to discover another passion: for each other. They corresponded all through the war and when Billy came home wounded, she helped him recover rapidly.

Billy had the same twinkle in his eyes as his father, and captivated everybody with whom he came into contact. He made people laugh with his anecdotes. He loved to talk, and his conversation was filled with information as well as with humor. He knew everybody from the corner bootblack to the president of the United States and treated them all the same, no matter their station in life. He liked people, and they instinctively knew it. Billy Phillips was, in short, much like his father, George Roosevelt Phillips.

At Harvard Billy had a friend who was improbably named John Smith, and, just as improbably, was black. In the Harvard of the late 1930s, this black John Smith was not accepted by some of his classmates. But the egalitarian Billy, like his father before him, introduced himself during the first class they had together, and they remained friends despite the unconcealed scorn of other underclassmen. For these snobs, however, the fact that a member of Billy's family had attended Harvard in every generation since its founding in 1636, made him the ideal champion of the new John Smith, whom he respected for his intelligence, humor, and strength of character. They had long, stimulating conversations. To Billy's surprise and delight, most of his other classmates were able to accept John too after about six months of Billy's friendship. Without exception, they all grew to appreciate him for what he was: an intelligent, jolly companion.

One night, after a particularly stimulating debate with Billy, John Smith went back to his room and died suddenly from an unsuspected blood clot, which penetrated his heart. Billy was devastated by this, his first encounter with death. It took him a long time to get over his friend's death. It was probably the reason Billy volunteered for the infantry instead of going into the Navy or the Air Corps or some branch of Intelligence, as did most of his classmates. Billy was determined to become so familiar with death that he could handle it on his own terms.

But he was no more prepared for another death in 1953 than he had been years earlier when John Smith died. Billy's father, having grown a bit portly over years of good living, became out of breath far too often. Against Sophie's advice, he continued to take his afternoon walks in Central Park. Although she loathed exercise, Sophie accompanied her adored

George on his strolls. One afternoon, he pointed at a tree branch with his cane and said, "Look, darling—" then slumped to the ground, dead, his statement unfinished. George Roosevelt Phillips, the old Rough Rider, canal facilitator, and *raconteur* died at the age of 75, revered and esteemed by all. Sophie was crushed. Closeted in their apartment, she died within a year. Everybody said she couldn't bear to live without George.

≈

After a few years in Washington, Victoria had charmed and impressed every person in the State Department; and Billy, although still a young man, had worked his way through many positions to become an advisor to the secretary of state.

Billy's leg, badly shattered at Omaha Beach, still caused him pain in cold, damp weather, and he limped slightly. When this happened, Victoria, in her quiet way, would hand him his cane at the door, admonishing him sweetly: "Here, dear, that leg of yours is being held together by a bunch of pins and needs to be looked after. Besides, the cane gives you a most distinguished flair!"

Once Billy laughed, "Honey, I was under the impression that I already had a distinguished flair."

Victoria retorted, "Dear, if you fall, it certainly won't be distinguished. But you'll need a flare to attract a rescue party, so take the stick!"

Victoria never coddled Billy, but was always there to anticipate his needs.

Billy frequently suggested to Victoria that they take a trip down to Panama. She never received the offer with enthusiasm, however. For one thing, she hated to travel. She was also scared. Every time she decided it would be safe to travel to Panama, Billy would come home with news about riots and turmoil, much of it aimed at the United States. She was not a coward but had no intention of getting killed just for the fun of it.

"When will this thing straighten itself out?" Victoria always asked.

"It's been festering a long time, Victoria. Back in 1936 Franklin D. Roosevelt increased the annuity we pay Panama to $430,000 when we went off the gold standard. The treaty stipulated we pay in gold, so we adjusted the payments to comply with our commitment."

"That's still a trifling payment! The Suez Canal Company paid a fortune to Egypt this year—over a million dollars more than we pay Panama."

Billy shrugged. "Different deal," was all he could say.

In 1955, Billy Phillips waved *The New York Times* in front of his wife. "Look at this!" he said. "Remember what I've been telling you? Well, it's happened. President Eisenhower and Panama's President Remón have signed a revision of the canal treaty. We're increasing the annuity from $430,000 to $1,930,000 and paying the Panamanians who work for the canal the same as we pay the Americans. What do you think of that?"

Victoria ignored her husband's question. "I've read the terms of the treaty already. It does not address the real cause of friction between Panama and the United States. I've been studying your father's notes. The Canal Zone was nothing but a land-grab. We just *took* it."

"They gave it to us by treaty," Billy said uncertainly.

"Nonsense. A Frenchman gave us something that wasn't his to give. What do you think this hostility has been all about? The canal? The Panamanians are delighted to have the canal through the Isthmus—but you've got to admit they should have received a fairer rent. No, dear, what's causing all the trouble is the Canal Zone, a foreign territory on sovereign Panamanian soil. It's insupportable under any conditions and you know it!"

"I still don't see why they blame *us*. After all, it was their representative who made the proposal. Bunau-Varilla is the one who offered to grant us sovereignty in perpetuity. We never asked for it or even conceived of such an arrangement. I believe poor Mr. Hay was as surprised as anybody when this Bunau-Varilla made his proposition. So now we get the blame. *We* are the imperialists. *We* are the aggressors!"

Victoria looked dubious, "You're right, but it still isn't fair."

Although the Treaty of Mutual Understanding and Cooperation went into effect, President Remón was not on hand to sign it. He was machine-gunned to death as he sat in his private box at the race track having drinks with friends after the last event. His death had nothing to do with the United States or with the treaties. It was a very complicated political murder. His assassin was acquitted four years later.

≈

Unexpectedly, due to unrest in Latin America, Billy was hastily nominated and confirmed as an ambassador in the area to help calm things down. Before leaving for his post, Billy insisted he have a bullet-proof car. After surveying the standard four door limousine, he called in the best security firm in the country to add several refinements to the sedan. It was now more like a tank than an automobile, and was impregnable. Billy wasn't worried about himself, but he knew he couldn't bear it if anything happened to Victoria.

≈

A month after their arrival, Billy and Victoria were on their way to a reception at the British Embassy. Without warning, a large truck came flying out of a side street, and screeched to a halt, blocking the main road. Three men in ski masks jumped out and began machine-gunning their car. The assailants were using armor-piercing bullets, which would have penetrated Billy's windows easily had he not taken the extra precautions. Billy remained calm, holding Victoria's hand. She was as steady as a rock. "What now?" she asked in a firm voice.

But Billy was already talking into the special radio phone. Two minutes later, the truck exploded, hit by a high-velocity artillery shell. The three assailants began running away, only to be seized by armed police.

Afterwards, the commander of the police peered in the limousine window. Without hesitation, Billy opened the car's door and congratulated the commander who saluted smartly. "Thanks again," said Billy.

"You will have an armed escort from now on, Mr. Ambassador. This will never happen again," the commander promised.

And it never did. Billy performed his job well without further incidence. The three attempted murderers were tried and sentenced to hang. In a grandstand play, William Phillips, United States ambassador and object of the assassination plot, officially requested the three not only be spared but also pardoned. This gesture changed the politics of the region from anti-American to wary neutrality in a matter of weeks.

Peace was restored. Soon Victoria gained the confidence of the local women when she established a children's hospital, a day care center, and a home for single mothers. Her projects changed the country's wary neutrality to active pro-Americanism. She achieved all this effortlessly, it seemed. Victoria and Billy made an effective diplomatic team.

As the wife of the American ambassador she was obligated to attend the usual diplomatic functions. During one such tea party, the conversation turned to the subject of relations between the United States and Panama.

"Don't you think that it is rather unfair of the Panamanians to treat the Americans so poorly after all they have done for them, building their canal, and eradicating yellow fever?" said Baroness von Bernuth, the German wife of the Argentinean ambassador.

Victoria took a sip of her tea, and placed it daintily on the table beside her. "Yes, Maria, you are quite right, the Americans have done quite a bit for the people of Panama, but I'm convinced that they have a right to feel resentful toward us. It is their country, and I believe that one day the canal should be turned over to them. After all, the other treaties we contemplated were only to be in effect one hundred years."

"Oh, nonsense, Victoria! You Americans will never allow that to happen."

"Well," said Victoria, "we aren't considered a patient people but perhaps the people of Panama are more impatient than we are. We'll just have to wait and see. Perhaps when England gives you back the Falkland Islands, we'll give the canal to Panama."

Victoria's remark effectively ended that conversation.

≈

After three years, the Phillipses returned to Washington with laurels. More important, Billy now held ambassadorial rank at the age of 40. The State Department had to make him an undersecretary.

That same year, 1959, Billy and Victoria followed another family tradition and had a son in middle age. They named him George Roosevelt Phillips in honor of his late grandfather. Billy and Victoria had never expected to become parents. Visiting Victoria in the hospital after the birth, one of Victoria's friends, the southern-born wife of a close Foreign Service colleague of Billy's, commented, "You all sure waited a long time before you decided to have a baby."

"We didn't *decide* to have a baby, Alma Sue. I assure you we had something completely different on our minds at the time."

≈

On the evening of November 3, 1959, a violent riot broke out in Panama. The United States embassy was stoned and the American flag was desecrated. Although only about one hundred fifty people were involved, the United States considered the affair serious.

≈

"Well," asked Victoria, "what are we doing about Panama?"

Billy stroked his chin, a sure sign that he was perturbed. "Discussions will be held, my dear, between our secretary of state, Christian Herter, and Panama's ambassador to Washington, Ricardo Arias."

"What's Arias like?"

"He's a very nice guy. Has been president of Panama. Became president after they shot Remón and is one of the few heads of state who actually finished his term in office. He comes from one of Panama's finest families, plays scratch golf." Billy had been gazing out the window as he spoke. Now he turned to Victoria and said, "He'll eat our people for lunch and not even burp."

"Why don't they put *you* on our team?"

"I'm too junior."

"You're lying, darling. I've lived with you too long to buy that."

Billy smiled. "They think I'm too sympathetic to Panama's cause."

"That, my darling, makes much more sense."

≈

Then, in Panama, on the evening of January 9, 1964, real anti-American riots broke out. They were fierce and bloody. The Treaty of Mutual Understanding and Cooperation specified that the American and Panamanian flags be flown together in the Canal Zone as an indication that Panama was still the sovereign of the area. At Balboa High School, an American facility in the Canal Zone, however, a group of students, of their own volition, tore down the Panamanian flag that had been flying alongside the American. Panama's flag should have been replaced immediately by the Canal Zone authorities, even if it had to be raised and guarded by American army troops, of which there was an ample supply. However, nothing was done. After waiting several days, a group of Panamanian students marched to the high school where they met a greater number of jeering, boisterous American high school children, backed up by their parents. A fight began. It escalated. American troops arrived to restore order. Tragically, a Panamanian student, Ascanio Arosemena, was killed.

From that moment, the battle became violent. Fourth of July Avenue, which marked the boundary between Panama and the Canal Zone, became a battleground. Buildings burned. American soldiers opened fire; Panamanians shot back. Looters robbed, and some of them were killed by gunfire or flames. According to the official count, twenty-two Panamanians were killed. There were probably more. Ten to fifteen U.S. soldiers lost their lives. There were hundreds of wounded. Panama's hospitals could not deal with the volume of casualties. The fighting lasted three days.

Diplomatic relations between the United States and Panama were severed. Barbed wire barriers were set up where, until then, people from both sides of the border had come and gone freely. Fourth of July Avenue was renamed Avenue of the Martyrs in honor of the Panamanians who perished in the fighting. Without a doubt, this was the lowest point thus far in U.S.-Panama relations.

≈

"What will happen now, Billy?"

Billy Phillips wiped his brow with a handkerchief, even though it was still January and their windows were slightly open. He shook his head, then said hopefully, "Ships are still going through the canal without interruption, I understand."

"No, they're not. A lot of the canal pilots couldn't get to work because of all the fires and the shooting."

Billy sighed. "You don't know the half of it, darling. The riot spread. On the Atlantic side of Panama, all hell broke loose, too."

"How did the Americans in the Republic of Panama fare? Were they slaughtered in their beds?" Victoria was practically in tears.

Billy shook his head vigorously. "No, dear. None of them were touched, from what I hear. Those who might have been were protected by their Panamanian friends. The focus of the mobs was strictly against the Canal Zone."

"Thank God for that."

By now Billy was pacing back and forth. "We still have no diplomatic relations with Panama. I wonder if we ever will again. There are plenty of communists around in that area, especially since Castro took over Cuba in '59. Don't tell me they won't take advantage of this."

Victoria looked pensive. "I don't think so. There are too many Panamanians who won't let that happen."

≈

After tempers cooled down, Panamanian and American diplomats began speaking to each other again. The upshot was a resumption of relations between the two countries in May 1964. President Lyndon Johnson pledged to begin negotiations immediately to replace the Hay–Bunau-Varilla Treaty with a new document that would be acceptable to the Panamanians as well as to the Americans.

Billy came home late on the evening of December 13, 1964. "Well," he said, "Based on the unanimous judgment of the secretary of state, the secretary of defense, and the Joint Chiefs of Staff, President Johnson is going to announce tomorrow the American decision to plan a new sea-level canal and negotiate an entirely new treaty with Panama."

"Hooray! Hooray!" shouted Victoria. "We all know the canal's too old and incapable of handling today's shipping. It's about time we did something like this."

"Amen," said Billy.

In June 1967 three new treaties were signed. The first abrogated the original treaty of 1903, reduced the size of the Canal Zone, and provided for joint operation of the canal. The second confirmed the United States's responsibility to defend the canal. And the third addressed the possibility of a sea-level canal to be built by the U.S. in Panama.

None of the treaties was ever ratified.

Oh, Billy," said Secretary of State Dean Rusk, after summoning Billy Phillips to his office one day in 1968, "Panama's new president is going to be inaugurated on October first. It's going to be rather grand. Parties, balls, a partial transit of the canal, all that as well as the inauguration itself. We have to be well-represented, and we think you should go as part of our delegation. Your family's historic diplomatic connections with Panama are impeccable."

"Yes, sir."

"But be careful. As you know, the new president is Dr. Arnulfo Arias. He was elected twice before, thrown out both times."

"Yes, sir," said Billy. "The first time was in 1941 and the people who ousted him had our help and support."

"Oh?" said Rusk. "I didn't know that."

"Yes, sir. He went to medical school in Germany briefly in the '30's and was openly pro-Nazi. With the war upon us, we couldn't allow a Nazi to be president of Panama. The canal was vital to the war effort."

The secretary nodded, then grinned. "I knew that, of course, but I wanted to know if you did. You did. You've done your homework.

"The second time he was removed was in 1952, after he dissolved the Congress, the Supreme Court, and replaced the Constitution. It was a pretty bloody affair," continued Rusk. "The National Guard had to storm the Presidential Palace, and there were a lot of people killed before they got him out, tried him, and banished him. Now, he's back and was elected by a landslide."

"He's very anti-American, I understand," said Billy.

Rusk was silent for a moment. Then said, "No. He's changed his attitude. In fact, that's why we want to send a top-ranking delegation to his inauguration. He's been hinting that he'll make a deal."

"About the canal?" Billy was surprised.

The secretary nodded. "Yes, but we want to make sure. He says one thing one day and something else the next. He can be very calculating. That's why I say, be careful. He'll charm you so thoroughly, you'll end up giving him the canal and half the United States to boot."

≈

Dr. Arnulfo Arias was inaugurated on October 1, 1968, amid great festivities. Although they had never met before, Arias gave Billy a warm *abrazo* and told him how pleased he was to meet such a distinguished diplomat from Panama's greatest partner, the United States of America. Had he been less impressionable, Billy would have considered Dr. Arias his best friend in the world. As it was, he left Panama with the distinct impression that an arrangement could be made with the Arias government that would benefit both countries. He also left believing that Arnulfo Arias was Panama's only real leader and would continue to be for a long time.

He reported this to the secretary. "Also, sir," continued Billy, "I do think he'll make a deal. Probably for the good of his country. You see, Arnulfo, as everybody calls him, knows that the Panama Canal is Panama's greatest asset. So, he wants to negotiate the best deal he can from his country's point of view. He knows that what we pay Panama every year is chicken feed. He will want a lot more from us. Probably a voice in the running of the canal as well. He knows the canal makes money. He also knows we charge the cost of Canal Zone schools, the police force, the customs, the post offices, the courts, to make the profits seem less."

"I think I have the picture, Billy. But tell me this: Will he be reasonable?"

Billy nodded. "I think so. He's very pragmatic."

CHAPTER

Twelve days later, Billy Phillips was summoned once again to the office of the secretary of state. Dean Rusk was perturbed. "Have you heard the news from Panama?" he asked without any preliminaries.

"Nothing in particular," said Billy.

"Well, I'm putting you into the network. You'll be working—as an equal—with the undersecretary for Latin American Affairs for the time being. Anyway, you told me Arnulfo Arias was erratic. You understated it. Yesterday, he summarily dismissed all the top-ranking officers of Panama's National Guard."

"Good God!" exclaimed Billy. "They'll take over the government. Arnulfo will be lucky if he gets out alive."

"They already have taken over. There's been a military coup, and the Guardia is looking for the ex-president with the intent of ending his days forever."

Billy caught his breath. "Who is the head of state?"

"There are two. Both are colonels. Omar Torrijos is one. Boris Martínez is the other."

"Where is Arnulfo?"

Rusk winked. "He barely made it to the Canal Zone—which has always provided a safe refuge for fleeing Panamanian politicians—and spent the night sleeping on somebody's desk. He'll get out, either by U.S. military aircraft or by ship."

"Well," said Billy, "there goes our deal."

≈

After things settled down in Panama, Omar Torrijos assumed the rank of general, and his co-conspirators were gradually sent, one or two at a time, to Miami, with one-way tickets. Torrijos was undisputed head of state.

"We've suggested to General Torrijos that he can now take the opportunity to approve the treaties made in 1964 and 1967, since there's no congress in Panama now to oppose them."

Billy Phillips listened to the undersecretary carefully. "Will he do that?" he asked at last.

Shaking his head vigorously, the undersecretary said, "No, he won't even consider them. If I may quote him, He 'has concluded that none of the treaty projects fulfill the objective of attaining the prompt elimination of the causes of conflict between our two countries, that they are not useful even as a basis for future negotiations!' How do you like that?"

"Not much," said Billy. "What he wants is the elimination of the Canal Zone."

"He won't get it," said the undersecretary. "Our congress would never stand for it!"

≈

"General Torrijos might be a dictator," said Victoria. "But at least he's a benevolent dictator."

"I guess he is, at that," said Billy. "But what makes you think that?"

"Other dictators, like Castro, for example, had all their opponents shot. 'To the wall! To the wall!' remember those words? To the wall and a firing squad. He killed thousands. The gunfire could be heard all night long. Torrijos just sends his enemies to Miami."

Billy nodded. He thought Torrijos was good for the country. What worried him was who his successor might be when the time came.

"I hear you're having an affair with your secretary."

Billy jumped, even though he was sitting down.

"What! You're crazy! Who told you that, for god's sake?"

Victoria and Billy were so close to each other, one could always tell when the other was attempting to lie. Victoria knew Billy was telling the truth. In fact, she couldn't even imagine him having an affair with any-body but her. Still, she arched her eyebrows and shook her head. "Well," she said, "You certainly haven't been as passionate with *me* as you usually are. I feel very deprived and neglected and—"

"I know, honey," he said. "I agree that we have some catching up to do. Between Panama, George's chicken pox, and everything else," he shrugged.

"Shut up and kiss me, you fool," said Victoria quoting a line from an old movie they both enjoyed.

≈

The next day Billy took his lovely wife, protesting, down to the office. "I want to show you off," he said.

After presenting Victoria to the members of his staff, all of whom she impressed mightily, he finally introduced her to his secretary. Mildred Brown was no match for Victoria. She was short and plump with straight, mouse-colored hair. Yet Billy's introduction made it sound as if he were presenting Victoria to Marilyn Monroe. Mildred beamed.

As he escorted Victoria to her car, he commented, "I can certainly see why you're jealous of my secretary. Believe me, I have to keep a tight rein on my passion. I try to be strong, but—"

"*Touché.* And a good one for you, darling," said Victoria as she blew Billy a kiss.

41

Early in 1971, after an informal meeting between the U.S. secretary of state and the foreign minister of Panama, which was held outside of both countries, the American representative offered to reinstate negotiations for a new canal treaty. Panama's foreign minister agreed, and the machinery was put into motion.

Billy Phillips was named as one of the advisors to the negotiators, and the meetings began that same year. By the end of the year, progress had been made.

It was then that Billy, back in Washington, had one of his very few spells of anger. Clutching a newspaper in his hands, he shouted to no one in particular, "Damn them!"

"Damn whom, darling?" asked Victoria, completely unruffled.

"Damn the damned Panama Canal Company! Read this. It says the Panama Canal Company has demonstrated that the present canal is far from obsolete and there will be no need for a sea-level canal before the twenty-first century."

"So?"

"So the negotiators for the United States are going to lose interest in continuing the meetings. They're happy with things the way they are. Why should they make a new treaty?"

"Ahh," said Victoria, "The canal bureaucrats are sabotaging the negotiations."

"You've got it, sweetheart."

≈

Panama was not to be outdone that easily, however. The Americans had never dealt with a man like Torrijos before. He invited U.S. negotiators to Panama for talks. He and they disagreed on every point. An official from the Canal Zone suggested that Panama should be grateful to the U.S., because without their assistance Panama would not have been born. To this, Torrijos shot back, "Being the midwife never gave you the right to rape the child!" The U.S. was confused and frustrated. The meeting ended in a stalemate.

After the American negotiating team returned, the secretary of state called for the Honorable William Phillips. After both men had sat down, the secretary said, "Billy, I want you to go to Panama and meet Torrijos. You're a good judge of character. I want to know what you think of this fellow."

"In what capacity do I go?" asked Billy

"Informal visit, but with all the credentials of my Special Envoy."

"Is there any hurry?"

"Hell, yes, there's a hurry! General Torrijos is taking this thing to the U.N. Security Council. And he wants them to call a meeting in Panama!"

"But, sir," said Billy, "it's a binational problem. Can—?"

"Yes, he can. We've opposed it on that basis, but nobody's with us."

42

William Phillips went to Panama, and immediately upon his return he reported to the secretary of state. The secretary sat back in his chair without saying a word. He was there to listen.

"I had several meetings with General Torrijos. Mostly at his country place or on Contadora Island. Always informal. He is a very handsome man, charismatic as hell. Popular as any leader in the world today. His people idolize him and will do anything for him. And he is brilliant. Good common sense. Handles people well. A natural politician. Couldn't be more astute. He's taken Arnulfo's place as undisputed leader of Panama."

"No faults at all, I suppose," said the secretary, smiling.

Billy laughed. "Plenty," he said. "For one thing, he likes to drink a lot. For another, he likes the girls. Doesn't care what age or marital status. He's insatiable. The Latin lover personified. He's not a good public speaker, if you analyze it, but his personality hides it. Sir, even with all his faults, you're up against a genius who makes Machiavelli look like a novice."

Little did they know that General Torrijos was just warming up. To put more pressure on the United States, he resumed diplomatic relations with Cuba. He did not make known the fact that he was, in reality, extremely anticommunist and detested Castro.

The United Nations Security Council met in Panama in March 1973 to deal with Panama–United States relations. On October 21, 1973 , the Security Council recommended that an entirely new treaty regarding the canal be negotiated; that Panama's sovereignty in all its territory be respected; that the Canal Zone be reintegrated with the Republic and the Zone under U.S. jurisdiction be dissolved with Panama assuming all jurisdictional prerogatives; and that the groundwork be prepared for the assumption by Panama of full responsibility for the operation of the Canal.

The resolution received thirteen affirmative votes. The United States opposed, and the United Kingdom abstained. Since the U.S. was a permanent member of the Council, this draft resolution was not adopted. However, these were, basically, almost the exact terms subsequently agreed upon by the United States and Panama in their final treaty.

Meeting followed meeting until in June 1976 a joint U.S.–Panama report on negotiations was presented to the General Assembly of the Organization of American States in Santiago, Chile.

In August 1977 the U.S. House of Representatives proposed legislation to express the sense of the House that the "U.S. Government should retain unimpaired its sovereign rights, power and authority and jurisdiction over the Panama Canal and the entire Canal Zone."

≈

"So, what do you think of the Congress's attitude toward the canal?" Victoria asked Billy.

"I don't know," he said. "But I do know that President Carter is about to announce that Panama and the U.S. have agreed in principle on the new Panama Canal Treaties."

Victoria was silent, thinking. "It's going to be tough, isn't it?"

Billy nodded. "But unless we concede some of the points that Panama considers important in the way of treaty revision, there's nothing to prevent Torrijos from simply taking over the canal like Nasser did Suez in 1956. And don't think every nation in Latin America won't back him up, either! Most of the rest of the world will, too. And there's no way we can use force to stop it from happening. When President Johnson said negotiations would never be undertaken under the threat or implied threat of violence, he didn't realize that applied to both sides. He was thinking only of the 1964 riots. Armed intervention of the U.S. now would be unthinkable."

"So, now *we're* the ones who have to make the best deal we can?"

"You've got it, darling."

≈

At breakfast the next day, Victoria was up and dressed. She usually let Billy have breakfast alone with his newspapers, then came down as he was about to leave the house, just to kiss him good-bye. "Up early, aren't you, dear?" Billy's words sounded casual, but his pulse was racing. There had to be a very good reason for his beloved to be up and dressed at this hour.

Victoria smiled sweetly. "Yes, my love, I have to catch the shuttle to Boston."

"Oh?"

"To see what I can do about George."

Billy put down his newspaper. "What do you mean? What's wrong with George?"

"Oh, nothing much, dear. He just wants to leave Harvard and join the Marines."

"What?" Billy jumped up from his chair, unintentionally knocking the newspaper onto the floor.

"Yes, dear. That's the way George imagined you'd take the news."

Billy stood still. "Look, I have nothing against the Marines. They're as fine a group of men as there are. But, remember, I was in the infantry and I know what George will be in for if any shooting starts. He'll be in the front of the attack. He'll—"

"Billy, dear, why do you think I'm going up to Boston?"

"You'd better let me go instead. I'll straighten young George out mighty quick."

"Your country needs you, Billy, dear. So, you just stay here, and I'll keep you advised."

"How is it possible that when he knows his father is engaged in the most delicate of negotiations on the part of our country, George Phillips decides to complicate things by leaving college and joining the Marines? I ask you, sweet Victoria, how?"

"I'm not going to tell any of our families I'm in Boston. I'll call you from the Ritz-Carlton just as soon as I've straightened things out. Bye, darling." She kissed him on the cheek. As an afterthought, she said, "And don't get involved with Miss Brown while I'm away. I promise I'll be back soon."

≈

Billy was earnest as he entered the office of the Commandant of the Marine Corps. They shook hands cordially. Then, without preamble, the Honorable Billy said, "General, I have a very small problem. I have a son at Harvard who wants to drop out and join the Marine Corps."

The general beamed. "Wonderful, Billy. We need good men, and if he's your son, he's what we want."

"His mother and I want him to finish college," said Billy wondering what the general's reaction would be to that one.

The Commandant of Marines leaned back in his chair and smiled. He pushed a buzzer on his desk. When the secretary answered, he said, "Please get me the Marine Corps recruiting office nearest to Harvard Yard."

The two men chatted until the buzzer went off and the general picked up the phone. The party at the other end was properly impressed. Billy could tell by the pauses when he was saying, "Sir" this and "Yes, sir" that.

"You'll get an application from a George Roosevelt Phillips. Please turn him down. Tell him he doesn't pass the physical requirements. Tell him anything. Understood?"

The general looked up. "Done, Billy? But I certainly hope you won't object if he joins up after he graduates."

Billy smiled and shook the general's outstretched hand.

≈

That evening, Victoria telephoned. Before she could say anything, Billy blurted, "It's done. The Marines will reject him. I saw—"

"Easy, darling," Victoria cut in. "I had a nice chat with George, and he's already decided not to enlist."

"So, when did this happen?"

"Before I arrived."

"Give me some details before I have a stroke," Billy pleaded.

"Well, dear, it's a long story. You see, George was madly in love with this girl up here. He's been seeing her ever since he entered Harvard, and I think, even while he was at Andover."

"So?"

"So she ditched our George and got herself pregnant by some star football player."

"Good God! And she wants to say it's George's?"

"Oh, no, darling. As a native, you will remember that here in New England people behave better than that. She and the football player got married."

Billy sighed with relief. "So why did George want to join the Marines?"

"He was heartbroken, you idiot. Then he remembered his grandfather going off to Cuba with a broken heart as a Rough Rider and you landing at Omaha Beach. You've simply got to spend more time with your son, dear."

Billy nodded at the phone. "How do things stand now?"

"All is well," said Victoria.

"Thank God," breathed Billy. "George stays at Harvard. He stays single. And he's decided not to join the Marines for now. I hope that's what you mean."

"Yes, darling, your quick mind never ceases to impress me."

"Do me a favor," said Billy. "Don't ever mention Omaha Beach to George again? Tell him I was a rear-echelon bastard for the whole war. Something like that, okay? And I promise you I'll spend a lot more time with him—just as soon as things settle down a bit here."

Victoria rolled her eyes at Billy's last remark, then said, "I'll be back tomorrow. Don't you wish you had me to solve all of your problems?"

CHAPTER

44

The treaty was signed by President Carter and General Torrijos on September 7, 1977 at the Pan American Union in the presence of representatives from twenty-six other nations of the Western Hemisphere. Negotiations had lasted thirteen years. Jimmy Carter knew he was taking a serious political risk. But he took it.

There was much congratulating and good will after the signing. General Torrijos in his remarks took occasion to say, "This repeals a treaty not signed by any Panamanian."

The new treaty was ratified by the U.S. Senate by a one-vote margin.

≈

Afterward, snug in their Washington study, Victoria asked, "Tell me in a nutshell, honey. What does all this mean?" She tossed aside the document.

Billy knew that Victoria understood but wanted to chat. "Well," he said, "in a nutshell, the U.S. Canal Zone will be eliminated completely. It means that over the next twenty-three years there will be a gradual transition of the control and operation of the canal from the U.S. to Panama. The canal will remain open to all vessels even in times of war. The final turnover of the canal to Panama will be December 31, 1999, at noon."

"But, Billy, Panama is so small. Suppose Russia or China decide they want it?"

"There's a provision in the treaty that if the operation of the canal is ever in danger, we can send in the troops and guarantee the canal's safety."

"Thank God for that. But, tell me, love, when are they going to build a sea-level canal?"

"Soon, I hope. Despite what the old canal bureaucracy says, we need it badly. But it's going to cost several billion dollars."

"How long will it take to build?"

"Oh, I'd say about six years. At least, that's what the Japanese estimate."

"So, if you take a couple of billion dollars a year, based on the United States's budget, we're talking chicken feed."

Billy was lost in thought. But he nodded.

"So, it's done," said Victoria.

Billy nodded. "As long as all goes well for the next twenty-three years, it's done."

Victoria smiled.

"What in the world are you smiling about?" asked Billy.

"Oh, just the irony of the thing. Just think, the most monumental, efficient and costly engineering project ever devised and completed by man will be given to one of the smallest countries in the world. Do you think they'll be able to manage and administer such a monster?"

"They'll have twenty-three years to learn. And the Panamanians aren't dumb. Most are unusually bright."

"For most Americans, having to turn the canal over to Panama must be painful," said Victoria. "I don't think it's sunk in yet. Wait until 31 December 1999, to be exact. How do you think they'll react then, when it actually happens?"

Billy shrugged. "We're like thieves who have to return our ill-gotten loot."

"You're blaming your great uncle, then."

Nodding, Billy said, "On the other hand, Panama, which is now taking possession of the canal, might never have emerged as an independent country. But it did. And we continued our inflexible attitude even more severely. For us to have accepted the Hay–Bunau-Varilla Treaty was like Eve accepting the apple from the serpent in the Garden of Eden. The temptation was just too great. In that treaty were sown the seeds of discontent, which were never swept away—perhaps until now."

"But, darling, you have to realize the Hay–Bunau-Varilla Treaty was signed in a different era than ours. It was the turn of the century, the age of imperialism and 'gunboat diplomacy.' Our country was simply playing by the rules that were in effect then."

"So, now let's play by the new rules and see what happens."

≈

Between the signing of the Carter-Torrijos Treaty and the actual turnover of the Panama Canal to Panama, quite a few events occurred, none of which had anything to do with the treaty itself.

General Omar Torrijos was killed in 1981 when his private plane crashed in the mountains of Panama. Naturally, conspiracy theorists attributed the crash either to Colonel Manuel Noriega, next in line to take over, or to the Cuban Communists. Then there was the obligatory theory that the C.I.A. was to blame. But Torrijos' death is, and has long been conceded to have been, simply bad weather—about which Torrijos had been warned.

Jimmy Carter was defeated in the 1980 elections, losing to Ronald Reagan, an avowed foe of the new Panama Canal treaties.

Panama went through trying times under General Manuel Noriega, mainly due to U.S. sanctions which hurt the anti-Noriega middle class most of all. The U.S. airborne invasion of 1989 removed Noriega, and Panama has been a working democracy ever since. Elections have been fair, and the results uncontested.

After Noriega's capture by the U.S. Army, the government was assumed by Arnulfo's old party, even though Arnulfo himself had died several years before. Afterward, the voters elected the party founded by Torrijos. The two main contenders in the 1999 election were Martin, Omar Torrijos' son, and Mireya Moscoso, the widow of Arnulfo Arias. It was not surprising that political parties founded by Panama's two strong, dynamic leaders, Arnulfo Arias and Omar Torrijos, continued to dominate Panamanian politics. In 1999 Arnulfo's widow, Mireya Moscoso, was elected president of Panama.

≈

Victoria and Billy Phillips waited uncomfortably in the new baseball stadium in Panama. They were pleased to be part of the American delegation at Mireya Moscoso's inauguration and to be among the crowd of almost 25,000 supporters of the first female president of Panama, but they had been waiting for nearly three hours.

"I wonder what's causing this delay," said Victoria.

"I'm not sure. Something or other the legislature has to pass on, I understand," replied Billy.

"Mireya doesn't absolutely control the legislature, does she?"

"That's putting it mildly," said Billy. "A couple of months ago, at a large meeting, her party members began talking about the difficulties the new president was going to have with the assembly. That was when one of her supporters yelled, 'Don't worry, Mireya, remember you have the people!'"

"So, Panama will have a woman president," Victoria said. "The U.S. has never had one, but 'macho' Panama has one now."

"Latin America has had more than its fair share of female heads of state," Billy retorted. "Argentina had Isabel Perón. Nicaragua had Violeta Chamorro, and I could probably think of some more."

Victoria shook her head. "No, you're right as always. What still bothers me, though, is whether Panama will be able to operate the canal efficiently—female head of state or not."

Billy answered without hesitation as the tumult and applause indicated Mireya's arrival and the approaching ceremony. "As far as I know, nobody doubts that they will be able to handle the canal just fine. The eyes of the world will be on the Panamanians; and, besides, they've already been running the canal efficiently for the past couple of decades. Unless the professional politicians stick their grubby little hands into the cookie jar, I think this will be advantageous to us all."

"I certainly hope you're right, dear. I think it's very right and fitting that the Panama Canal be replaced by the Panamanian Canal."

Before an audience of diplomats, heads of state, and leaders of government, President Moscoso became not only the first woman president but the first Panamanian to lead a *completely* independent Panama.

"At this moment," she proclaimed, "when we are about to end the century and our nation enters an historic era with the departure of a foreign presence, when we are ready with pride and dignity to usher in the new millennium with our sovereignty fully rescued, it is I, the first woman who has received the trust of the Panamanian people, who will take on the great responsibility of leading the nation."

≈

The first official call upon the president of Panama was made the next day by the American delegation, led by Janet Reno, the U.S. attorney general.

≈

As an aside, although he claimed his actions regarding Panama were meant only to restore the honor of France, Philippe Bunau-Varilla—the source of all the bitterness between Panama and the United States—retired an extremely wealthy man. In the First World War, as a major in the French Army Engineers, he performed valiantly until, in the late summer of 1916, a bomb blew off his leg. He lived a prosperous and happy life until 1940, when he died in his bed.